OLD HABITS

by
Ben Trebilcook

Printed by Amazon

Dedication
To Hans and Simon

Acknowledgements

For over twenty years I tried to get *in* on a certain action franchise. This is for those who liked my concepts and also championed me. My folks, mom for putting up with the sweary movies and more and Pops [a real-life McClane] - and my brother Steven. If I hadn't broke my entire left side BMX-ing, I wouldn't have been off school and you would never have rented me so many movies that made a tremendous impression on me. 'Young Guns' [thanks John Fusco] and 'Die Hard' on VHS in 1988. Also rented were a bunch of Ninja movies, 1963's 'Castle of Owls', Sho Kosugi's '9 Deaths of the Ninja', Michael Dudikoff's 'American Ninja' series and Beat Takeshi films, as well as a string of Hong Kong action thrillers; John Woo, Tsui Hark, Ringo Lam, thank you. 'A Better Tomorrow 2', 'City on Fire', 'Full Contact', 'Bullet in the Head' and 'the Killer' fueled my passion for Eastern cinema and when I was fortunate enough to meet John Woo in 1994, my love of 'Die Hard' and the Far East just had to meet. I knew I had to fuse the two together some how, with a sprinkling of Pop's own amazing dinnertime good guy and bad guy stories. Thanks to my Jen for always being there and re-arranging the plot in my 'Old Habits'.
Early days' thanks to my first agent, Paul Levine, Skip Brittenham, Andy Vajna
and my late manager, Jeff Ross.
Cheers to my talented filmmaking and journalist friends Phil Stoole, Tony Giglio, Reg Seeton, Sean O'Connell, Ken Napzok, Alicia Malone, Hiro Masuda, Mark Reilly, Clint Morris, Berge Garabedian, Garth Franklin, Eoin Friel at Action Elite, Jordan at Manly Movie, Sean Hood, Jeff Sneider, Amy Goldberg, Matt Hamby, Kristian Harloff and team Schmoes Know,
Neil Marshall, Johnny Sullivan, Stuart Heritage, Louis Leterrier, Ed Neumeier, Iain Smith,
Gail and John McTiernan, Ollie Diaz, Doug Richardson [always there for advice and positivity, thanks, mate], Steven E De Souza [inspirational wowzer] , Jonathan Hensleigh and

Roderick Thorp.
My very good friends; Designer Ben Hickman [being 'shot' by
Pop's finger-guns, kick-starting the filmmaking and coining the
phrase 'it's Moet Night' – cheers, brudda. Er.], Designer Ant
'Edith' Gardner [book covers are ace, beers with you are ace],
cheers to the super-talented and forever-supportive gang
Steve Simmonds, Jim Arnott and Dan Baines.
It's not a big book. It was based on an original screenplay of
mine, but you'll get the idea.

"It's gonna be hard to get in on that franchise." a producer
once said.
"I suggest writing your own." he continued.
Yippee Ki Yay.

4

CONTENTS

Acknowledgements

1. [one]

Ich Bin Ein Berliner

Wiry hands mixed soot and burnt tree roots in a chipped bowl. The hands belonged to a forty year-old Japanese man. He wore a green uniform, had a white headband and sat on a tatami mat. Around him were several other Japanese men, each of similar age and also in the same green garb.

They didn't look too healthy, but were alive at least, in the dark, damp, underground cell.

Bolts sounded out. They created disturbing echoes down corridors beyond the heavy door.

The metal door opened, accompanied by a piercing squeal of unoiled hinges, which alarmed the men inside.

A six-foot two European looking man was suddenly shoved inside the cell by four Japanese guards. He, too, wore a green uniform and one that was in a much healthier condition than those worn by the Japanese occupants of the cell. He was a muscular man. Well built and sturdy like an oak. He was fifty back then.

The man with the white headband locked eyes with the European and slowly got to his feet. He extended his hand towards him.

The European shook the welcoming hand, gently squeezing it with his large handed, gorilla-like grip.

Mister White Headband smiled a rotten-toothed grin and nodded his head several times. He gestured to the tatami mat and the other men sat and stood around inside. He was a little older than the European, but the years had taken their toll on his mind.

The European, with his deep-set eyes, scanned the room. He was extremely fortunate not to have to duck or crane his neck, as the ceiling was just high enough for him to stand upright and without having to hunch. He eyeballed the other men inside, eating their bowls of rice. He stared and recalled a painful, recent memory, which fueled him with rage.

Outside the Volksbühne cinema in East Berlin, the European man held the hand of his five-year old grandson. He was smartly dressed and rightfully so.

The Volksbühne meant 'theatre of the people'. It was built during nineteen thirteen and nineteen fourteen and designed by Hungarian-Jewish architect Osakar Kaufmann, right in the heart of Berlin. It had a slogan, too. 'Die Kunst dem Volke', which meant art to the people. This was engraved on the front of the building. It was a theatre for the working classes, designed for those to be able to access culture. During World War Two the Volksbühne was practically destroyed and rebuilt in the nineteen fifties.

A mousy-blond little boy, filled with glee and clothes matching in smartness to that of his grandparent. He looked up at the gigantic, statuesque figure beside him.

His grandfather was his hero. His rock. His guide. His official carer. His everything.

Ever since his father had died, he was looked-after by him. The boy was the beat of his grandfather's heart. He was the glint in his grandfather's eye. He sang Frank Sinatra's 'My Way'.

His grandfather had lost one son and was raising the boy as if he was his own child. He had another son, as well as a daughter, who he rarely had contact with. The European was born just before the Second World War broke out and seven years old when it had ended. He wasn't brainwashed by Nazis or fascists or any other racist, right wing group or anti-political movement. He, like his father and grandfather before him and when his sons were born and when his grandson was born, they were to be instilled by something much more important to them than a symbol or ideology.

Their birthright.

The prisoners along with their green uniforms aged and became worn over time. Their clothing was torn, frayed, scuffed and singed.

Beatings and mental torture had lessened since the European had settled amongst them. Perhaps guards were too afraid to punish or threaten him. Fearful of the giant's size and his amazingly well maintained physique. Or, perhaps, it was because time had changed and passed so quickly, taking with it an old way of thinking.

The European man narrowed his eyes and watched a guard through the bars change the batteries to a torch. He gripped the bars, as he watched the guards.

One guard suddenly jabbed him with a stick, shoving it into his cheek. He pulled back and cracked it down on his knuckles.

The European jolted and stepped back with shock, but he returned to his position, sensing his situation was about to change.

Another guard looked up and threw a battery. He threw another. It hit the muscular European in the neck and knocked him backwards.

Mister White Headband surprisingly caught his fall.

The European closed his eyes briefly and reopened. He nodded narrowed, grateful to his new friend.

Each man had different reasons for being there, but their pains were shared by all of them.

Outside the Volksbühne, the five-year old boy, who still held his grandfather's hand and who continued to sing 'My Way', widened his eyes with worry.

A screech of car tires sounded out. It was incredibly piercing as it echoed along the cobbled street.

The boy froze with fear.

Several masked men stepped out from looming shadows and suddenly grabbed the smart European. They dragged him to an awaiting nineteen eighties' made Mercedes' truck.

"Opa!" cried the five-year old boy. "Opa!"

A black cloth bag covered the muscular European man's head.

The men struggled this way and that and dragged the European backwards towards truck.

The heels and toes of his luxurious looking shoes became scuffed and instantly worn looking as he twisted and turned.

He was pulled backwards by the aggressive foes that had leapt from the darkness.

Within the underground cell, a worn black cloth was unrolled. It revealed an array of tools, made from sharp animal bones and fashioned bamboo sticks. Some had metal needles.

The European man watched the men inside as he sat on the tatami mat.

A prisoner held the thrown batteries. He moistened some sheets of toilet paper and began to bind the batteries end-to-end. He secured a wire at either end and looped it.

The European man could see the wire was frayed in the middle. He saw the wire heat up, like a lighter. He looked at Mister White Headband sat on a mat near by.

He was heavily tattooed, illuminated by the moonlight, which shone down through a hatch several meters above. He turned to see his European cellmate admiring his inked back.

The well-built European had replaced Mister White Headband on the moonlight mat and was having a traditional Wabori tattoo on his scarred back and buttocks by the wiry, aged man.

The tattoo was a cherry blossom.

Mister White Headband shaved the European's face and head with a razor.

Years passed by.

Mister White Headband was a much older man.

The European had much larger arms and was covered in beautifully drawn tattoos. A rising dragon and a samurai was inked upon his muscular back. The European watched a prisoner remove a shoelace and attach it to a short stick of bamboo.

He tied razor blades to the lace.

The European conducted press-ups within the cell with one of the other prisoners sitting on his back.

Mister White Headband was now seventy-years old. His uniform was ever so worn. He was haggard and loyal. He was the European's Man Friday and then some. He rarely spoke and when he did, it was more of an incomprehensible mumble. The occasional "Hai" was muttered, accompanied by his near-always nodding head. He inserted a needle under the European's skin. Though he had always wanted to introduce himself to the European, he found it difficult to even recall his own name. He couldn't remember. The years of torturous days and nights had taken its toll on his scarred mind. Mister White Headband was imprisoned for being a major player in the organizing of a protest rally, marching against a

US nuclear weapons base. He, like the European, was taken off the streets.

His mother and father would put up fresh 'missing' posters each week for twenty-five years until their death.

His girlfriend at the time, a fellow activist who managed to slip under the government's radar, continued the effort. Despite moving on romantically, she, too, would put his picture in shop windows and under car windshield wipers, in between raising her own family.

Her children would ask her about the man she referred to as their uncle.

She would tell them he was an educated, kind-hearted and loyal man. She told her children that their uncle was quiet when it was necessary to be silent and gave a loud voice to thousands when they found it difficult to speak out. She told them he respected all people from all backgrounds and that nobody was below or above them. She would instill this in her own children, too.

Mister White Headband was extremely knowledgeable of the past, as well as being a true visionary. He felt the painful loss of his family and beloved like a knife through his heart. Despite accepting his fate, he longed to have had the opportunity to say goodbye. He wondered why he had not given up and died in that underground prison cell, like other men he had seen. Mister White Headband came to the conclusion that it was the love of others that kept him alive.

Thunder suddenly boomed. It cracked the sky. Rain sneaked into the cell and water rolled down the walls. It was unpleasant and an unfortunate common occurrence which the men had become used to.

The muscular European gritted his teeth. He pained by the years of mental torture, loss of his family and utter discomfort. A lightning flash illuminated him.

A rat scurried across the uneven, cracked concrete. It avoided the occasional muddy puddle but was suddenly snatched by a bony hand.

A Japanese prisoner, in his sixties grabbed the rat. He shuffled backwards to a far corner of the underground cell. He looked completely nuts. His pupils were like slivers of black olives and as big as cue balls.

A similar looking man, who crouched on a worn tatami mat, picked ticks from his head. He occasionally ate one, discreetly, hiding his little treat from his cellmates, believing that if they saw him eating, they, too, would want a taste. He worked his jaw to grind his chattering teeth on the ticks.

The dark, damp, underground cell had certainly affected the majority of the men inside.

Their mental health was in urgent need of attention. Perhaps beyond any medical help.

A shadow dipped and rose several times.

The men heard deep, heavy breaths. In and out. In and out.

The men were mesmerized by the European.

A barbed wire fence surrounded crudely built, armed, wooden watchtowers, positioned on a cold field, in North East Japan. They overlooked grassy mounds, with metal lid-like hatches.

**North East Japan
Black Site: Unacknowledged Secret Prison
P.S.I.A. – Public Security Intelligence Agency**

A camouflaged masked white man appeared from underneath a grass patch within the compound.

Ffft!

Two watchtower guards were shot dead by the man's silent bullets.

The man scrambled close to the ground, towards one of the metal hatches, just as one opened nearby, to reveal a guard. He shot him dead.

The body jerked, like an electrical charge had passed through him.

Through his mask, the man stared at his newly created corpse, jerking before him.

Within the underground cell, the deep, heavy breaths stopped.

The rat holding man twitched and turned to his tick-eating companion. Together, they listened.

The other prisoners halted what they were doing and looked upwards.

An enormous thud was heard from above. Mud and dust sprinkled down.

Instead of weights, the frail Mister White Headband was being bench-pressed by the European.

He was eighty-years old now. His muscles were clearly defined through his faded green, torn uniform. His arms were huge. His hair was tangled and matted and his face bearded. He was built like Arnold Schwarzenegger. His name was Frederick. He raised the loyal Mister White Headband upwards and exhaled his warm breath into the cold cell. Mud fell onto his face. He listened and held the old Japanese man up. His biceps and pectorals flexed under the strain. Frederick listened. He formed a curious expression and knew something was about to go down. Frederick sat up and placed Mister White Headband gently down on his feet.

In the darkly lit corridor, underground, fluorescent lights flickered.

Japanese voices yelled out, accompanied by bursts of gunfire.

One guard bolted round and aimed his weapon, but it was too late. He was riddled with bullets, which ripped through his uniform, piercing his flesh and tore up his lungs and organs. The bullets cracked his ribs and he was forced back off his feet and into the wall. The guard fell to the ground in a blood-soaked heap

Frederick squinted at the tough metal door.

The sound of metal shells pinged against the door. A couple hit the cell bars.

The echoed screams joined gunshots and the occasional thud as guards were shot dead beyond the cell door.

Silent bullets penetrated the rusty, damp metal walls in the corridor.

The masked man shot two more guards. His heavy, black boots trod on the chest of one guard, as he passed them by. Blood and guts squelched as the boot pressed deep into the exposed chest wound.

Three crazed Japanese faces stared through a barred window to a cell door as he passed it by. They had suffered years of solitary confinement. Who were they? What was their crime? Even they had forgotten why.

The masked man applied an explosive gel around the tough metal door of Frederick's cell. It glowed and illuminated the dim corridor. He stepped back and waited several seconds.

All was quiet within Frederick's cell.

Frederick was wary and stepped backwards. He never took his eyes off the cell door.

Chomp! The prisoner with the rat suddenly bit its head off.

Fizz.

BOOM!

The door flung off its hinges and flew into the cell. It decapitated the rat man and embedded into the wall.

A bright light on the end of an automatic machine gun zipped this way and that. A red laser-sight beamed around the dark cell like a light-sabre.

The masked man entered the cell. His gun trained in every direction. He held it like a professionally trained member of a special-forces unit.

One crazy-eyed prisoner watched the masked man closely. He swayed. Hypnotized by the open doorway to potential freedom.

"Opa?" said the masked man.

The crazy-eyed prisoner jolted when a wounded guard stepped inside, brandishing a Remington 870 shotgun.

Frederick stepped out and with one hand he slashed the guard's face with a bootlace razor whip. With his other hand, he punched the guard out cold, snatching the shotgun in one swift motion. Frederick pumped back the shotgun. He turned and squinted at the masked intruder.

Mister White Headband stood behind them, along with the other prisoners.

One stared at the corpse of the rat man. He felt the situation was less dangerous now and so knelt down and picked up the half-eaten rat for himself. He brushed some dirt off the rat and began to eat it, occasionally looking up to watch the live stage show being acted out before him.

The white man removed his mask to reveal his mousy blond hair and a lean, handsome face. His name was Philip. He was thirty-five years old.

"My grandson?" said Frederick in perfect Japanese.

Philip smiled, curiously.

Frederick stepped up. He eyed Philip closely and smiled.

2. [two]

Brady

Two guys wrestled a Christmas tree outside Hackensack University Medical Center, in New Jersey.

The daylight was fading as a star was being fixed both on the tree as well as inside.

Within a room inside the medical center, an X-ray was slapped onto the wall. It depicted a shoulder joint.

The doctor was of Indian origin and was around thirty-years old. "OK, you can put your shirt back on and we can talk about this."

Joe Brady was cynical, exhausted-of-life and people. He sat, bare-chested, on the edge of the bed, in his boxers. His body was a road map of scars and burns. He was worn from bullets, cuts, scrapes and old stitches. He was unshaven. His hairline was heavily receded and what was left was gray and patchy. He didn't care and why should he? He didn't care too much about anything, especially fashion. Brady appeared trance-like. His eyes were glassy as he stared at the x-ray.

"Mister Brady? Detective?" said the doctor.

Brady rolled his eyes up to meet the doctor's. "I'm retired.

"Glad to hear it." the doctor turned to face Brady. "I said you could get dressed."

Brady glanced down. "Glad to hear *that*. Getting cold." He then turned his attention to his right elbow and saw two metal pins jutting out. He winced, whether with pain or at the sheer sight, it was uncertain. "Hey Doc? They staying there?"

The doctor placed another x-ray next to the first. It depicted a knee joint. "The pins are there so the bones heal in alignment. They stick out so the surgeon can easily remove them. We'll just cover them over.

Brady sighed. He buckled his belt to his jeans and pulled on a white wife-beater. He disliked that term. To him, it was simply a vest. He recalled something and chuckled, painfully, to himself.

"Which one would you like first?" said the doctor.

"This a good news, bad news type thing?" said Brady.

"Unfortunately, a both bad thing."

"I'm listenin'." Brady sighed.

The doctor pointed to various parts of the x-ray as Brady stared, taking in his words.

"Both your knees have depleted cartilage layers between the joints. Layers of cartilage exist at the point when the ends of two bones meet. We call that the joint. The healthy layer is called hyaline, which *you* have none of. It's causing your bones to rub together and cause you severe pain. Your left shoulder, the head of the upper arm bone was previously shattered. It's difficult to put the pieces of bone back as the blood supply to the bone pieces have been interrupted. What you're experiencing here is Avascular Necrosis. It's a painful condition that occurs when the blood supply to the bone is disrupted. There's also a huge tear in your shoulder."

Brady swallowed. He curled his lip, nodded his head and looked up at the doctor. "And in English, please, so someone like me can understand it."

The doctor looked Joe up down. He saw a humble man deflated, defeated even. He saw someone who wanted it plain and simple and so he gave it to him that way. "Your shoulder and knees are fucked."

"Head, shoulders, knees and toes. There goes my favorite nursery rhyme. Jesus." Brady nodded and pulled on his shirt.

"Osteoarthritis is a common condition of cartilage failure. It can lead to a limited range of motion and invariably pain and chronic fatigue." commented the doctor.

"Hey, L'Oreal? You can skip the science bit. What caused it?"

"Falling from buildings and fending off terrorists didn't help, but in my opinion heavy alcohol contributed most."

"There I was preparing for cancer." mocked Brady.

"Well, it has been known for blood cancers to be caused by metals leaching from the knee prosthesis over a long period of time and we will be testing for bone cancer."

"Christ. Do you people cure that?" asked Brady.

"If by you people you mean doctors, then yes. It's an evolving field in orthopedics. For your shoulder, I'd recommend replacing the joint with a highly polished metal ball attached to a stem and a plastic socket.."

Brady interrupted, sarcastically. "Waitminute. You sure it's highly polished? The metal ball?

A white cleaner mopped floor as the door opened.

In the corridor, Brady closed the door and walked slowly. He recalled the doctor's voice.

"There are replacement techniques. Cells are used to re-grow cartilage tissue in order to replace damaged cartilage. Some work more effectively on younger and healthier patients. Others use a fleece matrix where cells are inserted directly into the joint, but they're only available in Great Britain and Australia. I'd recommend replacements for both knees. It's routine surgery with a 95% success rate."

The cleaner discretely lifted Brady's fingerprints from the door handle and pocketed them into a cool, little box. He went back to mopping the floor as Brady rounded a corner.

Brady passed day-to-day hospital life. There were a thousand and one thoughts in his mind. He plodded towards the exit. "And if I don't have surgery?" he asked the doctor.

"Pain will become more severe. It'll interfere with everyday activities. Reaching into the cabinet, washing, toileting..'

"Toileting?" mocked Joe. He neared the exit and sneered.

"This must be incredibly hard for you. Do you have any relatives who you can stay with or tell this to? Perhaps a close friend?" asked the doctor.

Brady stepped up to the doors, which swished open to reveal an African American man in his late fifties.

His name was Jaynus Carter. He was a tall, wiry man and loyal to Joe, but boy was he angry. "I was at least expecting a fucking wheelchair!" Jaynus yelled.

Brady walked alongside Jaynus across the parking lot and lit up a cigarette. "C'mon, I needed a ride."

Jaynus scowled. "If you can walk down a corridor, you can walk to a cab stand. Put that cigarette out, man. I'm fresh out of pine trees."

Brady stubbed the cigarette out on the wing of a parked silver sedan and watched Jaynus pull a set of car keys.

"Brady? This is my car, you asshole. Stub it out on your damn face or do what normal people do and put it in the trash."

Brady sighed. "How d'you know I'd be here?"

Jaynus held up an iPhone. "Your voice mail message, asshole."

Brady eyeballed the phone as Jaynus opened the door and clambered inside behind the wheel. Brady wearily opened the passenger side and got into the car.

Jaynus inserted the ignition key and watched Brady wince with pain as he sat down.

"I didn't think I left a message."

Jaynus slotted the phone into the dashboard and scrolled to a list of voice-mails. He highlighted a name: 'Asshole.'

"I'm in your phone under asshole?" asked Brady.

"Oh don't feel special, Brady. Whole bunch of assholes in this phone. You're just the top one. Should feel proud." Jaynus shoved the vehicle into gear as the voicemail message played out.

"Fuck. Shit. Dear Mister Brady. Your re-scheduled hospital appointment will now take place yeah, yeah, yeah, at two-fifteen, Hackensack Med.-"

BEEP.

Brady was an experienced New York City cop. He had enrolled in the New York City Police Department during the sweltering year of nineteen seventy-seven.

There were a lot of firsts for Brady that year.

It was the year he met his wife-to-be. It was the year he saw someone die and it was the year he both fired his police-issue revolver in defence and killed someone when doing so.

The streets were his office and he thought that he knew them better than most, but what a time for him to join the NYPD. His first day would be his branding. To say it was a baptism of fire would be an understatement.

It was July thirteenth, nineteen seventy-seven. It was the day of the New York City Blackout.

Some believed it was the Russians using a powerful device to put their Cold War enemies into mass panic. Some thought the blackout was caused by high-ranking masons and government forces to test how citizens would react to a radiation outbreak. There were even those who believed it was the doing of serial killer, the Son of Sam.

The official explanation was that the New York City Blackout of seventy-seven, was caused by lightning striking a Consolidated Edison substation along the Hudson River.

At that time, the Big Apple was bankrupt. The City was in the middle of a ten-day heat-wave and needed power

That year, that night, every crime imaginable was about to take place.

Pop, pop, pop, pop. Streetlamps were blowing out, one by one, along the street like giant birthday candles. It was like a domino effect. When one line suffered and powered-out, the next line gained too much power and had to be shut down. It was a chain reaction and in no time, the city was had lost all its power – and not just with its electrical output.

In a Police Precinct on Broadway, a bunch of cops were casually milling around when a middle-aged guy burst through the doors.

The guy looked at the cops with sheer disbelief. "What the fuck are you guys all doing?"

Several uniforms turned and frowned at the guy and exchanged bemused looks with one another.

"Who the hell are you, sir?" asked one patrolman.

"Who the hell am I? I tell you who the hell I am, officer. I'm the guy telling you that they've taken every damn thing outta my store!" he yelled.

"Who have, sir?" the Commanding Officer, a Sergeant, asked, wearily.

"You think I can describe a hundred and one fuckin' people, Sergeant?"

The sergeant sighed and heaved his bulk up and round from his desk, grabbing his keys and meeting the gentleman. "Okay, sir, maybe you can show me what's going on, huh?"

When he stepped outside, the sergeant glanced down the street. He saw a burning trash can on one corner and shook his head at the sight of it. Turning, another flickering flame caught his eye on an opposite side of the sidewalk. It was another trashcan, burning in the night.

"Those there ain't the problem. They're on every goddamn corner, officer. What I'm talkin' about is up there! Look!"

The sergeant looked along the arm of the man to see where he was pointing. He widened his eyes with shock.

Broadway was in a state of chaos. It was an infestation.

Thousands of people, like ants, in formation, heading into their colonies, the stores on and off Broadway and leaving their formicaries with various goods.

The sergeant and the storeowner clambered into his patrol car and drove closer to the action. He was in utter disbelief.

"I don't believe it."

"Well believe it and do something about it cos it ain't doin' anybody any good." blurted the storeowner.

"I think it's doing them some good, don't you?"

A middle-aged couple carried a brand new sofa out of a furniture store and paused, like rabbits, literally in the headlights of the patrol car, gripping the edges of the sofa and staring directly at the sergeant behind the wheel. They exchanged a look and continued, hot-footing it across the street and into the darkness.

Returning to the precinct, the sergeant looked at the handful of patrolmen at his disposal. It was without question more officers were needed.

A New York City bus driver pulled up outside the Police Academy at East 20th Street between Second and Third Avenue, near Gramercy Park. Gray-shirted new recruits mixed with a range of serving officers.

The Academy was a ropey building to begin with when it was built in 1964. Over ten years on, it had become more tattered, along with its iffy wiring and hard to manage trainees in their cramped conditions.

Fifty to sixty officers were ushered onto the awaiting bus, many of them nervous as hell.

One officer was shoved six ways from Sunday as his fellow blue bloods filed past him to get on board. "Hey! What's happenin' here?" The officer had been a fully-fledged member of the Department for little over two months. Although he had gained the attention of a beautiful young woman at the World Trade Center in May that year, when a 'human Spider-Man' scaled the South Tower and was successfully brought down by police negotiators, the officer had experienced very little with regard to life-changing events. He had grappled a pot-dealing member of the Chinese Ghost Shadows gang, where he grazed his arm against the wall of a convenience store. He had slipped and bruised his knee, as well as his ego, when climbing a fire escape in pursuit of a purse thief and he had been verbally abused countless time. It was nothing compared to what he would witness over the next twenty-four hours. The officer being shoved around was, of course, the young Joe Brady. Naturally Brady had grown up in an authoritative household, with his father, Gerry, reeling off his own stories of policing in the city, but now it was his turn. Brady was told they were being transported across the city to various precincts to support those who urgently needed back up. "That's not my precinct. I'm based up in-" he was cut short and hustled onto the bus.

The doors swished to a close and the hulking metal pulled away, rumbling up the street.

It wasn't long into the journey when screams were heard, accompanied by gunshots.

Brady and several others jolted.

"Jesus, would you look at that."

Brady turned to see his friend and colleague Burt Lamb gesturing out the bus window.

"Black out! Black out!" came the cries of some zipping this way and that outside on the street.

"Oh, my God! That's my kid brother's teacher!" Burt Lamb blurted, pointing at a woman carrying a television set under one arm and a box of sneakers under the other.

"That woman there, she's a church leader in my neighbourhood!" shouted one of the new recruited sat at the back of the bus.

The bus made its first stop Down Town and a police Lieutenant poked his head inside.

"I wancha nightsticks in hand and guns cocked and ready to shoot. The first ten, get out here. Go. Go! C'mon!" he barked.

Brady was one of those ordered out of the bus. As soon as he stepped out onto the sidewalk the stinking air hit him.

It reeked of smoke. The air was clammy and stuffy and stifling hot, not to mention pitch-black.

Brady looked up and saw two buildings on fire, flaming orange in the night sky. He winced, his ears pained by the sound of sirens blaring from nearby streets. He gained a glimpse of swirling red and blue and headlamps as emergency vehicles raced past.

The bus stores swished closed and headed into the night.

The Lieutenant looked at the fresh young faces stood in complete shock on the curb. "Jesus. Look atchoo lot. Sesame Street was brought to you today by the letters O M G." he told seven officers to head inside the precinct and wait for further instruction, while he told Lamb, Brady and a third officer to follow his lead.

"Where are we going to, Lieutenant?" asked Burt Lamb.

"You and him can ride up with me. You can get in the unmarked, which'll be up front, ya hear?"

Brady and Lamb exchanged a look and followed the Lieutenant to the patrol car, while the third officer stepped to an unmarked sedan and clambered into the passenger seat.

"I don't care who rides shotgun. Decide between yers. What I do care about is whether you're able to defend yourself and watcha backs and more to the point defend me and watch my back!"

Burt Lamb looked at Brady and shrugged. He made his way to the rear of the patrol car and jumped into the back.

Brady pulled his nightstick, opened the passenger door and clambered inside, resting the stick on his lap.

The Lieutenant got behind the wheel and glanced at Brady tugging at the seat belt. "Oh there ain't time for belts, kid." he eyed up in the rear view at Lamb fiddling with his revolver. "How many rounds you got there, son?"

"Six, sir." replied Lamb.

"Six? What if you gotta shoot five warning shots?"

"Maybe I'll save that last bullet for myself, Lieutenant." mused Lamb.

Brady smirked.

"With jokes like that, you best off yourself now, son and give him the other five rounds. Prepare for bedlam, kids. Prepare for bedlam." the Lieutenant shifted the vehicle into gear and followed the sedan up the street.

The unmarked sedan drove up in front, whilst the patrol car followed behind. The sedan beamed its headlamps into various storefronts.

Some were empty, literally, too. All its stock and even shelving had been looted. Others had some severe activity going on inside. It was utter bedlam. Just like the LT said. Complete and utter chaos.

The unmarked car drove onto the sidewalk, right outside one store. Its headlamps were on full-beam, shining directly into the store.

"What do we do?" Brady asked.

"I guess we've gotta try and restore some order." replied the Lieutenant.

"How'd you expect us to do that?" replied the young Brady.

"Beats me, kid. Just follow my lead."

The officers exited the patrol car, stepping into the beam of the headlamps.

Like cockroaches, looters scurried out of the store.

Brady was surrounded as people from the neighbourhood suddenly raced towards him and past him. He looked to the Lieutenant, who was already holding his nightstick high above his head and striking it down with tremendous force.

Whack!

He struck again.

Whack!

If he didn't hit a looter head on, he'd turn and crack the nightstick round the back of their heads instead.

Brady saw heads literally split open like an egg, complete with the yolk that spilled out.

Cries of "Officer, don't hit me, please! I'm just doing what everybody else is doing!"

Whack!

The Lieutenant brought them down and out cold.

"Should we be arresting anybody?" Brady yelled.

"Who's gonna listen to yer? Him? Her? That guy?"

Whack!

It was no use. The looters pushed past.

Burt Lamb was elbowed in the face and knocked to his knees. "Ow! Jesus! Where did that come from?"

Brady bolted his head round to see Lamb on the ground and then saw him receive a knee to the face by a nineteen year-old youth clutching a TV above his head. "Hey!" Brady gripped his nightstick and tightened his mouth. He suddenly swung it round and made contact with the youth's neck.

The youth's neck folded and his legs buckled.

The television set smashed. Plastic and glass and exposed wiring lay on the sidewalk beside the fallen youth.

Lamb looked up at Brady and nodded his thanks.

Gunshots sounded out from the darkness a block away.

Brady and Lamb blinked. They turned to the Lieutenant whose gun was already tight in his grip.

He fired twice in the direction of the shots.

Blam! Blam!

He continued lashing out with his nightstick as if he were cutting away vines and ferns with a machete in a jungle. "You! You! You're under arrest!" he yelled at two youths carrying stereo equipment. "You! Stop! Stop!" he shouted at a woman carrying three boxes of sneakers.

"They're twenty-five dollar sneakers! You think I'm ever gonna spend that much on a pair of sneakers, officer?" the woman spouted.

The Lieutenant turned his attention back to the stereo carrying youths and cracked them around the back.

They stopped, blocked by Brady and Lamb.

"C'mon, man!" said one of the youths.

The new recruits, Brady and Lamb, handcuffed and hustled the youths into the back of the patrol car, while the Lieutenant put the stereo equipment into the trunk of the car, when he suffered a jolt to the back.

He turned to see an African American man carrying a television set and in one swift motion, the Lieutenant cracked his nightstick hard into the man's face, splitting his nose. "You scumbag piece of shit. Get this punk in the back here!" he ordered to Brady and Lamb.

"There's no room in the back, sir." Brady said.

"I'm not talkin' about the back seat, asshole. Get him in the trunk and we can head back to the station"

The new recruits looked at one another, nodded and grabbed the man.

"Hey, man!" he lowered his TV, which the Lieutenant took from him.

Brady and Lamb tumbled the man into the trunk.

The Lieutenant dumped the television on top of him and slammed the lid down. "OK, back to the station."

"Then what, sir?" asked Lamb, twisting and avoiding a herd of looters.

"Then what? Then what? Then we start over, numb nuts. Move ya self. C'mon. Go. Shift it."

And so, they each got back into the patrol car.

"This is insane, man. You can't let all these folks go and round us up. That's just unfair!" protested one of the youths in the back of the car.

"You shut ya mouth, ya hear me, boy?" shouted the Lieutenant as he started the car up once more.

"We have a ten-thirteen. Repeat, ten-thirteen at West fifty-ninth on Seventh Avenue. Officer down." came the voice on dispatch.

Brady froze. The call of a ten-thirteen meant that an officer had been shot in the line of duty. It instantly made him think of his father when he was shot, especially as it was near to where it took place, too, by the park.

"Kid, you OK?" asked the Lieutenant, glancing at Brady's pale face and blank expression.

"His father was a cop and shot near the park." explained Lamb, leaning forward, cramped between the two handcuffed youths in the back.

"Your dad was a cop?"

"Yeah." Brady replied.

"Maybe I knew him. What's your name, kid?"

"Brady, sir. Joe Brady."

The Lieutenant stepped on the gas and headed back to the precinct.

Brady stared out of the window, passing more burning trashcans, broken windows and streets of madness, filled with looters. He craned his neck to see some teenagers ripping metal gates from a music store.

They grabbed hold of stereo equipment and musical instruments.

A passer-by tried to stop them, but he was beaten unconscious.

"You can get anything you want!" a young woman shouted in the street, holding two boxed blenders.

"Oh my good God." said Lamb as he noticed a couple of guys driving a brand new Buick out of a car dealership.

"Shit! Why didn't we think of that?" said one of the handcuffed youths.

Looters with sofas appeared from a surrounding block.

"Damn marauders. Look at 'em. All of 'em." commented the Lieutenant.

They continued to drive and push through the city.

Radio city management offered stranded patrons to stay inside. Some five hundred people took them up on their offer.

The handcuffed youths were put in the cells at the Lieutenant's precinct.

He was told there was no more room to hold any further prisoners.

"They're gonna open up The Tombs." one officer informed the Lieutenant.

The Tombs was a nickname for the Manhattan Detention Complex. It had been closed since 1974 and prisoners were already complaining of rat bites.

"Shoot! Shoot dammit!" came the Lieutenant's order for Brady to fire his weapon in the early hours of the morning when they saw a female fitness fanatic out for a jog being dragged back on her heels to an alleyway by two Puerto Rican men.

Her screams were disturbingly piercing and her fearful gaze locked onto Brady.

One attacker had a knife.

One had a .38 snub-nose, who noticed Brady and fired twice, before grabbing the woman by the hair and heading deeper into the alley.

Brady gripped his weapon with both hands and took aim.

BANG!

He discharged his weapon.

The Puerto Rican was his hit, dead center, between the shoulder blades. He went down like Jello, in a loose lump by a dumpster.

The knife-wielding attacker stood still as he gripped the woman's arm. "Get back, pig! Get back! I'll cut her throat, you hear? I'll do it!"

BANG! BANG! The Lieutenant fired his own gun, taking down the attacker cold. "How dare you. How dare you!" The LT yelled. His voice echoed down the alleyway.

The woman broke down in tears, thanking the officers.

The Lieutenant nodded his head and hugged the woman tight, gently pressing her cheek against his chest. His shield glistened upon her face.

New York City was a disaster zone.

Muggings.

Sexual assaults.

Theft was pretty much a given.

Arson.

The list was endless and went on and on that night.

There were over three and a half thousand arrests made that night. The damage caused was estimated at around three hundred million dollars. There were well over a thousand fires.

Around six hundred police officers were injured.

Brady observed his city. It was heart breaking to see such destruction. Such lawlessness and disrespect towards, well, everything. His arm ached from the swinging of his nightstick. He was exhausted.

For five years, in the late nineteen seventies, he had patrolled those streets. The idea of promotion and rising through the ranks didn't appeal to him, despite the continued efforts of those who looked out for him. The ones who tried to make him reconsider. Something was changing in his world.

It was the rise of the nineteen-eighties.

Pop-culture, technology advancements and Yuppy-dom were settling in.

Brady tried to keep rock alive and held on tight to his Creedence Clearwater Revival LPs. Punk Rock had quickly melted away, too and New Romantics and the jacket and T-Shirt combo wearing Slick Ricks had quickly replaced them.

Gangs, however, were ever-present.

New Money was there.

Cocaine was the in-drug of the wealthy.

It was the 'If you want it, go out and get it' decade.

The streets were getting more dangerous and tensions were rising all around him.

Brady knew that if he wanted to make a change, he had to make a change, too and so, he took the exam and was made detective.

Janus' silver sedan was parked outside Brady's apartment.

Inside the communal hall Jaynus watched Brady grip the handrail ascend the stairs.

He was pained by every step he took. He glanced down from the top of the stairs to where Jaynus was stood.

Jaynus sifted through the post inside the pigeonhole. "When d'you last sort your mail, Brady? Shit. Coulda won the lotto for all you know."

"Like you'd tell me. C'mon up." Brady continued a few more steps.

Jaynus eyed over a creased local newspaper dated fifteenth of July. It was folded to page five with a headline that read: 'HERO COP CELEBRATES 30 YEARS IN JAPAN'. Beside it was an old ID photograph of Brady from his NYPD day. Jaynus waved the newspaper and yelled. "Hey! When d'you go all big in Japan?"

Brady muttered to himself. "Why didn't I get a ground floor apartment? Huh? What was that?"

"Newspaper article? You in Japan?" Jaynus called out and bounded up the stairs.

Brady reached an apartment door and fumbled with his keys. His hand shook as he did so. His hands pained him, too. Arthritis had settled in two years prior and he still hadn't got used to it. "I didn't. I mean I haven't yet."

Jaynus stood outside while Brady struggled with his door, jangling the keys. Jaynus glanced at Brady's hand. He would never mention it. He knew Brady wouldn't want to discuss it anyway. It would only lead to an argument. If health-related topics ever cropped up in the news or in general conversation, that concerned somebody else, only then would Jaynus slip in a mention of Brady's own issues. "Talking of which, you could get that shaky-hand thing sorted out." Jaynus would say, only to receive a mumbled reply from Brady. Jaynus read the newspaper article: "Governor of Tokyo, Honzo Kimura, commented "Joe Brady should not have put the lives of others in jeopardy. His actions were reckless and fool-hardy."

"That was a long time ago." Brady replied.

"Yeah, thirty years." answered back Jaynus.

"Lotta scars and no shrink or relationship cured 'em." Brady held his look on Jaynus.

Brady could remember the night as if it was yesterday. It was an event that changed his life.

His wife at the time was fast becoming a powerhouse within the Far Eastern firm where she worked. She was zipping here, there and everywhere, barely having a moment for Brady. It was rare for a woman to progress through the ranks in an Asian country, but she wasn't in an Asian country. She was in the United States.

Brady had just been promoted himself. He was a Detective Lieutenant in the New York Police Department. It wasn't the job he thought he'd do, but he felt compelled to follow his own father's footsteps into the force.

Gerald 'Gerry' Brady was born in nineteen fifteen. The Brady family, first-generation Irish Catholic settlers, lived in Brooklyn. Gerry started his working-life early along the docks, mixing with various undesirables and learning how to survive on barely-nothing at all. The docks, at the best of times, were more than a little cutthroat and Gerry was fortunate to quickly gain a job at one of the many factories, producing glue and pencils. He had hooked up with Ewelina, a Polish Jewish girl who used to work in a neighboring garment factory. Gerry's factory began a sideline in producing beer and he started to earn some extra dough, however it was quickly spent on the drink that he was actually making. Gerry got pissed up on beer as much as the African-Americans and Puerto Ricans who came to Brooklyn in thousands pissed him off. "It's because of that damn train line!" he would yell. He moaned about the extension of the A Train running from Harlem to Brooklyn. "Jesus, Red Hook should now be called 'Black Hook' and don't get me started on Greenpoint. Those fecking people are taking all our jobs." he blurted.

Ewelina fell pregnant and she and Gerry soon became man and wife. The pair left Brooklyn for a brief stay in Queens and a chance-meeting with a fellow Irish couple on the street, associated to The Emerald Society, led Gerald Brady to join the New York City Police Department. It was his calling. He was truly proud to be called a New York Irish Cop.

The Jesters were a predominantly white gang and feuded with a mixed-race gang by the name of Egyptian Kings, who joined forces with another gang to become the Egyptian Dragons. Tensions had risen dramatically over the past several weeks and on the thirtieth of July in nineteen fifty-seven and forty Dragon members attacked five Jester members, brutally killing one boy of fifteen, Michael Farmer, in Highbridge Park, in Washington Heights.

Michael Farmer had polio since he was ten years old and walked with a limp. He was apparently not affiliated with any gang. Michael and his friend, Roger McShane, were mistaken for being members of the Jesters as they crossed into Dragon territory. It was the height of summer and temperatures were continuing to soar, not to mention gang-related violence.

The Egyptian Dragons were armed with Garrison belts, machetes, pipes, sticks, knives and homemade clubs. One member even used a dog chain as they entered the park to seek out rival gang members. Together they beat and stabbed Michael Farmer to death, severely injuring his friend, Roger, who took over three months to recover from his injuries.

Gerry Brady was one of the arresting parties two days later. He was disgusted by this senseless act and more so by the fact that three Dragon members were acquitted. It was the longest trial in the city's history, lasting fourteen weeks.

Two Egyptian Dragon members were convicted of murder in the second degree and two were found guilty of manslaughter in the second degree. Out of the eighteen who were rounded up, just four were found guilty.

Michael Farmer's father, Raymond, was a fireman in the city. "It's a sign to juvenile delinquents that they can get away with murder. These marauding savages have made a laughingstock of the law." he said, commenting that he thought the jury were too merciful.

It secured Gerry Brady to the bottle, but he vowed to clamp down on gang crime in his beloved city. The drink would never affect his work ethic. It was part of it back then. However, he would swear it wouldn't be an issue for his own children, Joseph and his newborn sister. He would study the sheets of handwritten information on the teenage gang members, noticing they each had issues surrounding the father-son relationship. He would even compile his own chart in the event that he would one day write a book on the subject. Gerry would interview members of gang after gang, from the Viceroys to Seven Saints, from Red Wings to Egyptian Dragons, Python Knights, Chaplains, Leonard Street Boys and Jesters. From Bishops to Hellburners, the vast majority had a negative relationship with their fathers.

"My father beats on me every time I open my mouth." said one Seropian member.

"My old man, before he kicked the bucket, whipped me and my old lady, then he'd demand his dinner and have his shoes shined, all before bedtime, which is when he would molest my kid sister." commented one Mau Maus gang member.

Gerry never wrote that book, but he swore he'd never beat his kids and tried to be a positive role model for them, especially Joseph, who idolized his father. One night, an off-duty Gerry was out visiting a friend and decided to cut through Central Park. He wasn't put off by the fact that his route may very well have him enter Dukes gang territory. "It's my city and I walk where I damn well please!" he would bark at his wife, Ewelina, concerned for his safety. What he didn't expect was a chance meeting with the East Harlem Dragons.

One Dragon, sat on a bench, flashed a sawed off shotgun as Gerry strolled past.

"Play safe, kids or ya mothers will be pickin' ball bearings outcha for weeks."

The Dragon was pissed at Gerry simply for being in the way of his intended target, a group of Dukes, pulling their own firearms.

Gerry soon found himself in the middle of a gunfight. Caught in the crossfire, he pulled a thirty-eight, concealed in his jacket and dove out of the way, rolling awkwardly into a railing. He winced with agony and dropped his revolver.

Bullets and the cries of the wounded sounded out.

Gerry scoured the concrete path for his gun. He saw it by the feet of a fallen East Harlem Dragons member.

His foot twitched and blood escaped his side, trickling along the path towards Gerry's revolver.

Gerry reached out for his thirty-eight and noticed the gang member looking down his legs at him.

"Yo. Yo, man. Help a brother out." said the East Harlem Dragon.

"Ya made ya bed, pal." replied Gerry, taking hold of his gun.

"Honky-ass motherfu-."

BANG!

An unseen gang member who lurked in the shadows shot the gang member in the head.

Gerry, wide eyed, knelt on the concrete and tightened his face. He squinted into the darkness and took aim, but nobody was there.

BOOM!

The shotgun blasted from nowhere.

Gerry ducked.

The sound of fleeing footsteps echoed into the night.

Gerry straightened and slowly got to his feet, but toppled over in an instant. He tried again, confused as to why he couldn't stand upright. He placed a hand onto the nearby railing to steady himself. He suddenly cried out in pain. "Ah, Jesus!" Looking down, he noticed his leg had been shot clean off below the knee. He was a bloody mess. "Oh you sons of bitches. You God damned sons of bitches!" Gerry yelled. He fired all six rounds into the direction of where the heard the footsteps.

A faint "Oh shit, man" blurted out into the night.

Gerry lowered his gun and glanced at his missing leg. "Oh for Christ sake. Jesus, Mother and Joseph. Oh Joe. I'm sorry, son." Gerry lost consciousness.

A car thief, with a conscience, feeling safe to step back outside, heard Gerry's moans and drove to Saint Luke's Roosevelt Hospital. The thief, claiming he simply broke into the car to hide from gunfire, was actually rewarded by the Police Department for his bravery.

Gerald Brady had little choice than to retire on ill health. He became bitter and drank more.

The event had a major impact on the young Joe Brady and like his father, he, too, enrolled into the New York Police Department.

It made Gerry proud.

A different city had arrived. Drugs were the main issue and heroin and cocaine flooded New York City.

"Half of me is glad to be out of it, half of me wants to fight 'em all. When oi think about it, half of me ain't even anywhere at all." Gerry mused at the changing times and his very different life.

His aging wife and young daughter would work hard and take care of Gerry.

It wasn't just the career path Joe mirrored, but also a love of alcohol. It was the main reason behind his separation, though Brady would say otherwise. He would blame scumbags and corrupt officials and his passion for a safer New York City. He wasn't a hero, by any means. In fact, he was extremely reluctant when it came to danger.

People would tell him the most dangerous thing he did was to smoke cigarettes.

Brady rarely took in the executive talk his wife would comment about at the dinner table or over the phone. It went above his head. He was an analogue guy in what was to become a digital world. He liked his simple pleasures: a beer, a pack of smokes and TV.

His wife travelled the globe. From face to face client services to setting up operations in Eastern Europe and overseeing the transition of rival buy-outs in Australia and the Far East. She would travel to Taiwan, the Philippines, Singapore and Japan. She was reliable and sought-after. She was the go-to person within the company whenever anyone wanted assistance, advice, thoughts on a particular aspect of the business and even a general chitchat with a coffee.

As the company grew, so did she and so their marriage - apart. The company began as a shipping corporation, but quickly expanded into trading, then employee engagement and benefits and then onto various technologies, communications and services. From banking to electronics to airplanes and automobiles to medical care, the company had its finger in many pies. They were innovative. They were the pioneers and led the way in so many different fields. They became a super-brand. When the company bought a globally recognized rival, it was indeed cause for celebration. It also meant Brady had to be invited to the party.

Brady felt it was a prime opportunity to repair his marriage and give it one last shot.

He took up his father's religion and became just another Catholic cop who kept a rosary in his locker and a picture of Mary next to his Beretta and shield. He didn't care where the corporation's party was, only that he had to catch a plane to get there. Brady disliked planes and above all, heights. When he was a rookie cop, he once had to climb a fire escape near the tenth precinct in order to catch a purse thief.

The thief almost got away, too, because of Brady's seven-minute hesitance to ascend the wall ladder.

"Whacha waitin' fwor!" shrieked the victim of the purse snatch. "You want *me* ta go afta him instead?"

The plane journey was swift and in no time at all he was stood outside the Oshiro Corporation.

It was the tallest building in the city and was undergoing a refurbishment. It was part office, part bank and part shopping mall. There was a lot of wealth housed inside, too. High-priced jewels and antiques to super-cars and of course, cash. It was a company and building that was certainly ahead of its time.

Brady hated parties. He was nervous. He thought about his wife and how he longed for a simple, perfect life.

The party was in full swing.

The Oshiro Corporation CEO was Yoshinobu Kita. He was a visionary and such a kind-hearted soul. Kita was tragically killed by a man who led a mixed group of murderous thieves.

They hailed from various factions around the world. Their common interest was killing and stealing.

The man in charge was an anti Robin Hood and his men were definitely not merry.

They were savage. They shot, bombed, raped and stole their way through every floor of that building that day.

Brady was shot, stabbed and blown up, too, but he was the reluctant hero. Unlike his father, he didn't want to get involved in such terror. However his passion and not wanting to let him or indeed his own family down drove him to become a force to be reckoned with. He was a man in motion. Brady rescued one hundred and thirty six hostages that day. He also killed the leader of the terror group who besieged the Oshiro building. Brady, in a prototype Oshiro sports car, shot dead the man, simultaneously driving into him, ramming him through walls and windows, tearing his body apart in the process.

His name was Alexander Mueller and was of German origin. Mueller, a well-spoken man was also privately educated. Why he chose the Oshiro building to rob was anyone's guess. It was as good as any, one would suppose. The lure of diamonds and gold was something else, as was his ultimate demise, but come on, he had a wife and young child to support!

For a few years, Brady's marriage was rescued, too.

Sarah and Brady raised a girl, Eve and later, a boy, Ben.

Danger, however, followed Brady wherever he went. He could have done the simplest task, like posting a letter and bam! He'd be in an armed siege. He once fixed a satellite dish on a roof and came face to face with a guy on angel dust, wielding a fire axe. It took twenty-eight rounds to bring that guy down. It didn't help matters that Brady fell through a skylight and cut himself to shreds in doing so.

He looked at Jaynus and recalled a brief memory of how they first met. It was another not-too-pleasant time.

Jaynus became embroiled in a suspected terrorist plot off Broadway and both he and Brady found themselves bonded by blood from there on.

Coincidentally a close relative of Alexander Muller led the terrorists and their intended loot had strong links to the Oshiro Corporation. It was an incredibly stressful time for both of them.

Jaynus underwent counseling. It took a lot of strain on his relationship, too.

The Lower East Side bars listened to Brady's woes.

That was little over twenty years ago and they had been 'friends' ever since.

Brady didn't really have anybody who he felt could be called a friend.

A couple of cop colleagues who would do him the occasional favor and vice versa and then there was Jaynus.

Jaynus was an equally miserable, yet loyal and reluctant to get involved in a dangerous situation kind of man. Well-educated in electrical engineering, his life-goal was put on hold, permanently, when his young wife was shot in the back and subsequently paralyzed by a stray bullet.

The bullet was discharged from a police officer's revolver.

The incident led to a race riot in Harlem.

The police officer who had shot Jaynus' wife had been involved in two similar controversial incidents just over a year prior to that one where he had killed a teenage boy. He claimed the boy, believed to be breaking and entering an apartment, pulled a gun when challenged by the officer. He was shot twice. The first shot entered the boy's neck. The second bullet hit the boy square in the back. The boy was also an African American.

The boy's death hardly made a dent in the press.

The second incident, concerning the officer, had him blind a bartender. One evening after work, he had turned up at an old school speak easy and was already drunk when he arrived.

The bartender asked him to leave, which led to an argument between them and a couple of locals.

It wasn't the fact that the officer was drunk. He could hold his liquor as good as the next cop. It was the fact that the bar was a Harlem establishment, meaning back then it was a bar for black people. The officer, indeed, had himself an issue with race. Although his name derived from Irish origin and despite the efforts of many a true said word on immigrants, he stood firm on his ignorant, bigot-views and continued to ramble on about them. The officer was a racist. He acted despicably and put a glass into the bartender's face.

The appalling act was hushed by those in power and despite a fine and a slap on the back of the hand by his superiors, the officer's job as a serving police officer was never uttered once by the court.

The officer's uncle was a politician. It helped greatly.

It was the man who made Jaynus the bitter, police-resenting, conspiracy-believing individual he indeed became.

"Good-riddance, racist-ass, murdering motherfucker." Jaynus said when seeing the announcement of the officer's death to liver

failure recently in a local newspaper. Jaynus'
dream of becoming a pioneer in engineering
was demoted to running an electrical repair
store in Harlem. He adored his wife. He adored
his family. He adored Harlem. His dream faded
away and attending the store became his life.
Jaynus looked at Brady, gesturing, impatiently
for him to open the apartment door.

The apartment was simple and untidy. A
TV/VCR combo and VHS tapes scattered
about the place. Some were labeled
'JEOPARDY' in black marker pen. There was a
sofa with a pillow and a blanket. There were
dishes in a sink awaiting a good clean and a
pile of post in need of urgent attention on a
work-surface.

Brady opened the fridge door and
peered inside, just as Jaynus spotted a black
envelope.

Jaynus slid an invitation on quality paper
from within the envelope.

Brady bolted and reached across the
post. He winced with absolute agony. "Would
you fucking put that down?"

Jaynus put on his glasses and read the
invitation as Brady tried to reach across again,
accidentally swiping some post to the floor,
revealing Beretta 9MM pistol underneath some
letters. Jaynus glanced at the gun. "What? You
gonna shoot me in your own apartment?"

"It's a Federal Offense to open
somebody else's mail." said Brady, staring,
seriously pissed off at Jaynus.

"Fuck you." replied Jaynus.

"Black man in a police officer's home."

"Fuck you, Brady. Place already looks like shit. Fit me up with a burglary, too while you're at it." Jaynus moved away to read the invitation. "On behalf of the Oshiro Corporation and the Tokyo Metropolitan Police Department, it should be our most humblest honor if you would grace us with your presence at our headquarters in Tokyo - shit - in receiving commendation for your outstanding efforts and valuable contribution in saving the lives of one hundred and thirty six Oshiro employees. Please celebrate the thirtieth anniversary with us and the decoration you truly deserve."

Brady swigged a bottle of water and popped an Aspirin. "You finished?"

"Hell no. Thirty years. Shit. You save over a hundred people when that lactic acid fermented cabbage-eating asshole tried to steal some Jap dough and you shun an accolade people save all their lives for. You are going to this, right?" asked Jaynus.

"Nope."

"What? And why not? You can't be doing your hair.," joked Jaynus.

"Ha-de-fucking-ha. I got nothing to wear."

"Now that I do believe. So what is it? Feel you might cry an' shit? Get all sentimental and nostalgic for a time long gone? Surprised they even want you there with your insurance history."

Brady sneered and popped another Aspirin. He tilted his head and dug into the drawer. He found a clip and slotted it into the 9MM. "It's a long way to escape Thanksgiving."

"But not for some surgery." Jaynus quipped.

"The fuck you talkin' about?" Brady scowled.

"On the way here. Told me your surgery can be done in Australia. You're an idiot, you know that? You fly halfway round the world. Might as well go that little bit more to receive your prestige. Got two plane tickets. Take one of the kids. The favorite one"

"There isn't a favorite one, besides, I don't think either of them wanna be reminded of their traumatic child-hood."

"So get in contact with their mom."

"Not necessary." Brady formed an 'If I go, you could go with me' look.

3. [three]

Oshiro

A commercial appeared on a twelve-inch screen. It depicted all walks of life on an everyday street. It was glossy and everybody shown had brilliant white teeth like fridge doors.

A Western businesswoman walked towards the camera. Japanese language was heard, however English subtitles appeared over the imagery. "At Oshiro, our highest priority is her."

A mixed group of Benetton-like teens ate and were seen hanging out. The voice-over continued. "And them."

A male tourist posed for a photo against a famous landmark.

"And him."

An elderly Japanese woman had a cushion puffed up for her in her chair within a care home by an African American nurse. She handed the elderly woman a PC tablet that depicted the OSHIRO Corporation logo.

"And her."

A mixed-race baby was cradled in a hospital bed by its smiling white, model-looking mom and its handsome and tanned father.

"And him."

A group of super-smiley people gathered together.

A kid was shown being home-schooled.

A cool bridge was depicted.

A mature, glamorous businesswoman addressed the camera. Her name appeared. Sarah Kita. She was white, in her late fifties and it stated that she was an Executive Vice President of Marketing at Oshiro Corporation. Sarah spoke perfect Japanese. "In fact, it's everybody on the entire planet. We've grown from being a Financial Services company to an internationally recognized brand. With our virtual learning home-schooling and advanced microchip, holographic and laser technology to our large scale construction projects, like our recently completed suspension bridge in Indonesia, we are committed to providing an excellent service, to every one of our customers and clients, but also promise to connect the most remote people in the world and give them a sense of belonging in being part of an altogether environmentally friendly global village."

Google Earth style imagery appeared on the screen. It showed a town, an ocean and then a huge landmass. The camera pulled upwards to reveal Earth and finally outer space.

"Sea, air, land.. Space. Wherever you be. Be Oshiro." Sarah continued.

Brady switched off the Oshiro screen that he just watched and reclined in his seat, on board the Boeing B777-2.

The plane was readying itself on the runway.

Brady shook his head and sighed. "Jesus. A reality star now?" He had just watched his ex-wife on that screen. Nothing would surprise him anymore. He had seen it all.

He had met Sarah when he was a young officer in nineteen seventy-seven.

A routine call, for Brady, regarding a possible B&E at a New York modelling agency led to the discovery of a dead body and a foot pursuit of a suspect who left the crime scene.

Although Brady gave chase across the busy traffic-filled streets and downtown back alleys, the suspect got away leaving Brady open to the banter of the NYPD locker room.

During that pursuit, however, Brady had written off his car. He crashed into a young, female office worker, who was heading to a job interview.

She found herself with a coffee-stained blouse and a strong dislike towards New York's finest, specifically one in particular. "Great. A total write-off! Just like my blouse! Thanks. Thanks a bunch." she said.

"Your blouse? Try not drinking coffee at the wheel next time." Brady snapped.

"Next time? I can't afford to have a next time, you jerk." Sarah responded. She was working in an office in the World Trade Centre in nineteen seventy-seven. Sarah much preferred to be in the crisp, May sunshine than be cooped up on the seventy-fifth floor.

George Willig, a mountain-climber from Queens, had scaled the South Tower.

A couple of cops, in a window-washing basket, were sent to get Willig, but soon discovered he wasn't a threat. They even had Willig sign an autograph for them.

Sarah and her colleagues were more than a little shaken up by 'The Human Fly' and his stunt that day.

Despite being afraid of heights, a young rookie cop took it upon himself to console Sarah. That cop was, of course, Brady.

Brady was a rookie uniform back then. He plucked up more courage asking Sarah out on date than he did leaning out of the window of that once awe-inspiring tower.

Sarah's no-nonsense, Italian father approved of Brady.

He saw a similar passion in him as he did within his daughter.

Both Brady and Sarah had a go-get-em attitude.

Sarah had a thirst for success.

Brady had a thirst for nailing scumbags. He also had a huge thirst for alcohol.

A pretty Japanese member of the cabin crew assisted the seat for Jaynus' lengthy frame.

Brady was tense. His ears perked up when he heard a passenger near by ask for a whisky and soda. The thought crossed his mind, but he fought it, like he had done for the past twelve years. Brady was upright. He was hung-over when he first met Jaynus. Brady looked across at Jaynus being offered a glass of Champagne. He saw Jaynus' exposed feet on a rest.

They were both in the comfort of Business Class.

"Thank you. Um, arigato." Jaynus said.

"Great. Gonna spend thirteen fucking hours staring at your dogs."

"It's called getting comfortable. You do your fisty toe bullshit or whatever the hell it is and I'll do what's best for me. These dogs bite, so watch yourself neighbor."

Brady sighed. He turned to his window.

The plane's engine began to roar. The Boeing B777-2 jetted across the runway and lifted off into the sky. Pasted across its side, accompanied by its logo, big and bold, was OSHIRO AIRWAYS.

4. [four]

Kura Sasori Kai
(Black Scorpion Association)

Eleven heavily tattooed naked men relaxed in a bath, within a Tokyo bathhouse. Their ages ranged from forties to sixties.

One man was the Governor of Tokyo. His name was Honzo Kimura.

The men were all yakuza and part of the Kura Satori Kai.

Honzo Kimura was the Oyabun. He was the family boss. "The Kin Kaminari Kai has become too powerful. Their corporation dominates every aspect of industry and trade."

One old Yakuza perked up. "What do you suggest? Derail their trains? Bomb their aircraft? We are ninkyo dantai not terrorists."

"Kumicho, we cannot start a war." commented another.

Kimura nodded his head when the men look up, alerted by the presence of other men.

Philip, naked and tattooed with a Kanon Bosatsu, the all-seeing Buddhist deity on his back, stepped close to the edge of the bath.

The men became alarmed even further.

Frederick, also naked, entered the water with Mister White Headband, who started to shave Frederick's beard.

Mister White Headband whispered to Frederick.

Frederick stared at the two yakuza that passed comment. Frederick smirked. He started to sing the opening lines of 'My Way' in Japanese.

Philip smiled and continued the song in both English and Japanese.

It was eerie and made the men feel uncomfortable.

Except for Kimura. He knew they would be there.

"Your gaijin advisor has gone mad." mocked the first yakuza, gesturing towards Philip, who walked around the edge of the bath.

Philip slid an HK P7M 13 pistol from under a towel. He had wanted this particular gun for a very long time and managed to get it, from of all places, on Ebay. "In the land of karaoke, the Japanese man is King. Sing with me. Sing! SING!

Men in the bath jolted with shock. Two bravely sung the words in English.

Philip rounded the bath. His tattooed butt-cheeks towered behind the bemused yakuza. He was threatening and intimidating as he ran the barrel of the gun over the shoulders and necks of the men. "Come on! This is like dairy-oke! You have to milk a song for all it is worth! Do you have regrets? Any of you?"

More men began to sing the tune. They were nervous.

Frederick watched on as Mister White Headband took great care shaving his beard.

Philip continued to sing, nearing the yakuza that passed comment. He suddenly tightened his mouth.

BANG! He shot one in the head. Blood and brain spat across the tiles like a Jackson Pollock painting.

Silence.

"What? Would you have preferred Gangnam Style?" Philip mused. He then conducted a brief Gangnam Style hobbyhorse dance.

BANG!

The men jolted with shock.

Philip shot the other yakuza in the neck.

Blood spurted across the tiles, skimmed upon the water and over the faces of some of the men.

The man tried to stop the blood by clutching his neck, pressing, hard and desperately.

Another bather tended to him.

"Leave him! He's dying." Philip said in perfect Japanese.

"He's an injured animal. Put him down!" Frederick commanded.

Philip pressed the barrel of his pistol hard against the man's temple.

BANG!

Philip shot the man in the head. "The two men were traitors to the Kura Sasori Kai. Loyal only to Kin Kaminari Kai. For years they have been your enemy. Your rivals. I can help you destroy them, leaving their name worthless and for the Kura Sasori Kai to be victorious once more."

"At what price does your assistance come?" said an old yakuza.

Philip and Frederick exchanged a look.

5. [five]

Brief

The distinctive dome-shaped 'Bubble' of the headquarters' auditorium of the Central Intelligence Agency was sited in Virginia. To be more precise, it was Langley, McLean, Virginia, USA.

In a briefing room, a collecting of male and female suits sat around a boardroom table.

The Assistant Director, who headed the table, loosened his tie and looked at a handsome young man.

The young man was raised mostly by a Mexican nanny and a far-too-busy business-headed mother. He had a father too drunk and absent to care about himself, let alone a couple of kids. He had, however, followed his father into a police career, but had bigger ambitions. Ben was a sought-after young man. He was extremely driven, but like his father, he had flaws. He didn't express his feelings. A handsome buck, well-built and like a Terminator, he was machine-like. Old-fashioned. It was in his genes to be distant. He was his father's son through and through. He was Ben Brady, the son of Joe Brady.

"OK, Europe, what do you have?" asked the CIA Assistant Director.

A female agent spoke out. "MI-6 is monitoring two home-growns who they're particularly concerned with in London. They recently became radicalized at school. Their family came from the Calais Jungle, which is an insane haven for the good, the bad and the ugly, mostly bad and ugly. France and Spain, no change. Minor migrant occurrences there. The situation in Greece and Turkey I'm following up on later. Other than that, nothing we don't already know."

"Asia?"

A US-Korean agent referred to his notes. "A Black Site for PSIA in Japan was infiltrated four weeks ago."

"Four weeks and we're just getting Intel now? Anyone extracted?"

"A member of the Japanese Red Army, a yakuza that couldn't remember his own name. One guy who conducted a sarin attack and an eighty-year old European."

"What do you have, Ben?"

"Apart from elderly watch? Erm, Eastern Europe, Russian FSB discovered another talking rock outside one of their government buildings. British intelligence actually owned up to that one."

Ben's phone vibrated upon the table. He discreetly slid it from the top and checked it.

The phone depicted a Tweeted scan of a baby.

"Quiet day then, Ben?" quizzed the Assistant Director.

"Huh? Oh, it was a Tweet. A baby scan picture. My sister. She's pregnant."

"You hacked her phone?" frowned the Assistant Director.

"Oh no! There'd be far too many texts to read." Ben joked.

The briefing was exactly that, brief and the agents gathered their paperwork and digital devices and left the room.

Ben Brady looked at the baby-scan picture once more. He smiled as it dawned on him that he would be an uncle soon.

6. [six]

Tokyo Streets

A light bulb dangled from a ceiling in a cellar of a bar where one would expect to get seriously messed up in.

An attractive woman in a short skirt and t-shirt sat in a dentist-type chair. Her wrists were clamped to the arms and electrodes attached to her temples.

Philip was impeccably dressed as he stood before her. He grasped her face and stared into her eyes, hypnotically. "When the gun fires, you saw a Westerner. Do you understand?" he let go of her and stepped back next to a towering, smart Frederick.

The woman received an electric shock. Her head and body jerked in the seat. Her eyes rolled upwards, revealing just her white eyeballs.

Frederick looked at the woman's fingers flexing. He glanced around the dimly lit room as the woman shook, violently.

She looked possessed.

The light bulb flickered.

At Tokyo's Narita International Airport, the Oshiro Boeing B777-2 touched down onto the Tarmac. Heat rippled upwards.

The plane turned and was soon fitted with a walkway.

The orange setting sun glowed like a fireball in the distance.

Brady was tired and unshaven as he exited with Jaynus.

Jaynus pushed a cart with two wheeled upright cases on it.

Brady caught sight of a digital Oshiro advertisement and two name-card holding suits ahead of him.

DETECTIVE J Brady flashed on a digital tablet that was held by a heavy-set Japanese man whose thumb was missing. Underneath Brady's name were Japanese kanji.

Brady made his way towards them.

Jaynus spotted the second suited guy holding a tablet with his name on it. "Look! I got my own digitized name, too!"

"Real happy for you, Jaynus. Hi, I'm Joe Brady."

A Bentley awaited them outside the airport where a flash of scarlet cloth caught Brady's eye.

A stunning Japanese woman called Mei wore a red dress and a white coat. It was hard to guess her age, as she was so incredibly doll-like. She could have been eighteen or she might well have been thirty. Her smile was brilliant as she greeted Brady and Jaynus who were led by the suited men. Mei bowed. "Youkoso irrashai mashita, Detective Brady. Welcome to Japan!"

Brady was taken aback by how beautiful she was. "Back at you. I think."

"Youkoso, Mr. Carter. Welcome."

"Hello." Jaynus said, politely. He was in awe of the place. As a man who loved technology and who worked in with electronics, he had always dreamed of coming to the Land of the Rising Sun. Home of technology.

"My name is Mai Kita and.."

"Kita?" frowned Brady.

"My grandfather was Yoshinobu Kita." replied Mei.

"Sorry." Brady apologized.

"I never had the honor to meet my uncle, but the family and corporation both mourn and celebrate him equally. His legacy and vision lives on daily at Oshiro Corp."

"You work at Oshiro?" asked Brady. Mei gestured the pair of them to the Bentley. "Most of my family does. Please. Goro will be your driver and accompany you to our hotel."

"Our hotel? You live there, too?"

Mei passed Brady a business card with both hands and a smile.

He looked at it to see it was digital. Thin like card, but depicted the Oshiro logo and scrolling text, contact numbers and an image of Mei.

"Nothing is as it seems in Tokyo. Anything you need, no matter how large or small. If it is to your need, it is for us to serve. Do not hesitate to call. It's a fun prototype for your stay here in Japan. Just press the Oshiro button."

Brady eyed the card, fixing on the Oshiro logo button. He squinted to see tiny scratch-like lines. It was a microphone. The card doubled as a cellphone.

Goro, the heavy-set, thumb-less suit, opened the door to the Bentley.

Mei handed Jaynus a business card cellphone, too.

Jaynus studied it. He was amazed and proud to have his own one. He bowed awkwardly.

"And a guest of Detective Brady is also a guest of Japan."

Goro eyeballed them both as Brady and Jaynus got into the vehicle. He closed the door and rounded the car to the driver's side.

A black and gold Kawasaki W800 SE roared up.

Mei turned and formed a disappointed look as the rider removed his helmet.

Jaynus toyed with his card and peered out of the window of the Bentley Flying Spur. "Looks like she's taken for, Brady."

Brady craned his neck and instantly took interest.

The bike rider was known as Masato. He was a handsome young man, with hair bodied like a stallion. Nothing out of place. Masato was a cocky fixer. He was a go-between who could mediate for a number of yakuza groups and politicians and businessmen alike. He clambered off his bike and stepped up to Mei in two lengthy strides. "We had a date. Did you forget? What are you doing?" Masato spoke in Japanese.

"I'm working." Mei turned, but Masato grabbed her wrist.

Brady stirred inside the vehicle as Goro heaved his bulk behind the wheel, eyeballing him in the rear view.

"Let it go, Brady." Jaynus sighed.

"Think you know me, Jaynus?"

Goro fixed on Brady and started up the car.

Brady stared at Masato gripping Mei's wrist outside the car.

"Nobody has to know you, Brady. They can see it written all over your Les Miserables face. Loosen up. Take one of your chill pills." Jaynus was relaxed, but was still his ever-cranky self.

"Chill pill? That whatcha call it?" Brady was pissed off.

"You want me to call them by their pharmaceutical name? Don't go sending me on another guilt trip."

"That was this is?" Brady sighed and took in the sight of the Kawasaki bike. He looked away.

The Tokyo streets reflected upon the Bentley as it drove along.

Brady and Jaynus stared out at the garish neon of Soapland. They saw the hostess bars, Thai hookers, stall-owners, love hotels, motorcyclists, cyberpunks, suited guys and Oshiro advertisements on digital billboards.

This was indeed Tokyo.

The Bentley stopped in traffic.

Brady yawned and looked out. He frowned as he saw the Kawasaki motorcycle owned by Masato. His attention was then drawn to a cop in a doorway.

The cop was being roughed up by a couple of hoods. One of them was Masato.

In no time at all, Brady had exited the car! He raced out and fought hard to ignore the pain of his aching bones.

"Brady!" yelled Jaynus.

Brady beat one of the hoods into a corrugated shutter. The metal clanging noise sounded out like thunder. He conducted a two-punch combination to Masato, knocking him out, cold.

Jaynus jogged from the car, but it was too late.

Brady looked at the cop.

His name was Ken. He was in his forties and was both thankful and disappointed. "That was not a good idea." he said in English.

"You speak English?" said Brady.

"You looked English, so I spoke English."

"Why wasn't that a good idea? Cop gets beat up, I'm gonna help out."

"They're Gokudo. Kin Kaminari Kai." said Ken.

"What you talking about?"

"Gokudo. The ultimate path."

"Huh?" Brady was confused. He didn't get it.

"Yakuza. They are yakuza." Ken said, looking at the knocked out Masato beside him on the ground.

Brady eyed the bodies around him. "Ninja bullshit?" he mocked.

Ken sneered and padded himself down. He pulled a pack of Wakaba cigarettes and offered it to Brady.

Brady nodded and popped a cigarette between his lips as Ken handed him a disposable lighter.

"What the hell is in your damn medication, Brady?" cried Jaynus.

Brady lit the cigarette. He discreetly winced with pain. His body ached.

"Are you all right?" Ken had noticed Brady's discomfort.

"Huh? Yeah. Just feel like the fuckin' Tin Man." replied Brady.

Ken suddenly straightened and bowed to a man that walked briskly past.

The man was Governor Honzo Kimura and he continued to walk.

"You got time to bow? These men attacked you. Call for backup." Jaynus said.

Brady glanced at Goro, who leaned against the driver's side, disappointed, but patient.

"That was Governor Honzo Kimura." said Ken.

"Honzo Kimura? That guy who won't attend your commendation?"

"That's him, huh?" asked Brady, who, in complete pain, decided to jog after Kimura. He rounded a corner of the street.

"Brady! Where you going to?!" yelled Jaynus.

Brady was out of breath. He reached Kimura and tapped him on the shoulder. "Hey?" Brady jerked Kimura around. "Hey! We need to talk? Foolhardy and reckless? That what you said?"

Governor Kimura looked Brady up and down. "Too busy to talk to tourists. Sorry." His voice was gruff. Kimura was pre-occupied with a world of other crap. He shoved Brady aside and paced away.

Brady exhaled his smoke. He watched Kimura merge with the crowds of suited salary men who plagued the streets. Brady, too, became one amongst the neon kanji. "Shit." He looked around his surrounds. "All looks the fucking same." He squinted and suddenly he cast his eyes on Kimura. He fixed on a row of XXX bars.

There were a lot of damn people. They shuffled along, close together, but never once bumped into one another. It was as if they had sensors, like cars.

Brady narrowed his old eyes on two men.

One of them was clearly packing heat.

Brady pulled his cellphone business card. He hesitated and thought for a moment.

An oversized neon bullet scrolled across the outside of a building of the same name; NEON BULLET. It was a hostess bar, one of the more upmarket ones, too.

Two attractive women stood outside. They were smartly dressed in black, though their skirts were a little too shirt.

One was Japanese.

One was a blonde Australian. She gestured to a woman dressed as an Anime character bopping around outside a rival bar opposite. It was then that a couple of businessmen approached them and the two girls put on their paid-for smiles and allowed familiar touching by the obviously recognizable men in suits.

They led them inside.

The Neon Bullet was decked in lowlight and gold leaf. Statues and round couches and planetarium mirrors adorned the place.

Masato sat on one couch. His arms stretched out straight on the upper edge, like he was nailed to a cross. He was pissed off and was having his bruises, ego and manhood serviced by three hostesses. He looked up and saw Philip, towering in front of him.

Philip had an SLR camera around his neck. He stared at Masato.

"Can't you see that I'm not into boys?" Masato said, turning away to look at one of the girls. He stroked her hair.

Two heavies stepped up either side of Philip.

The blonde Australian woman approached him and smiled a fake one. "I'm afraid pictures aren't permitted here, especially of this gentleman."

"I don't want to take Masato's picture. I want to take a photograph of former New York Policeman, Joseph Brady."

Frederick stepped into the light. He looked handsome, smart and slick. His large frame gained him the attention of everybody in the place, hostess, heavy and punter alike.

All were in awe of his presence.

"When he is lying dead in the morgue." Frederick added.

Masato waved the heavies away. He looked at Philip and Frederick curiously. Who were those foreign men that stood before him?

7. [seven]
Smart Building

The bridge extended from Tokyo Bay.
The Bentley Flying Spur drove across.
Brady sat alone in the back. He eyed the water either side of the bridge and then widened his eyes at the awesomely impressive sight.

It was an island where the Oshiro Grand Plaza was based.

Brady's mind raced. His left hand began to shake. Was it the drink or nerves? He wasn't sure. A drink would have stopped the shaking. It usually did. With his right hand, he gripped his left, tightly.

The Bentley pulled up outside the Grand Plaza. A door opened and Brady clambered out of the car.

Despite it being a different country, he felt he had been here before. Brady looked up at the amazing structure. He stared at the glistening, golden plaque on the wall. OSHIRO

GRAND PLAZA. He was tense, concerned and regretful. He tried to keep the violent memories at bay. 'Shit."

Jaynus stepped up beside him. Didn't get too lost to find your own Bentley I see."

"Dial O for Oshiro." Brady quipped.

Yoshi Kita welcomed them with a smile and open arms. "Gentlemen. Welcome." he said, leading the men inside the lobby.

"It's like being inside a fucking iPhone." sighed Brady.

The lobby had LCD flooring, ceilings and windows. There were Mobile Concierges with digital tablets. A touchscreen display mounted in a pillar brought up Brady's face as he walked past it.

"Good afternoon Mister Brady. It's an honor to have you be our guest here at Oshiro Grand Plaza. You must be tired. I suggest a personalized shower and massage before dinner." said the Robot Concierge.

"Yeah, yeah, you had me at Log In." Brady

"Good afternoon Mister Carter. Welcome to the Oshiro Grand Plaza." said the Robotic Concierge.

"What, no personalized message? How's that machine know it's me any how?" frowned Jaynus.

"It's state of the art facial recognition software. The building knows where you're going before you do. It scans global newspaper articles, social media, electoral roll, and motor vehicle registries. It even knows your music tastes. A Smart building." replied Yoshi.

"So where's the off button again?" Brady asked.

"This is turning my floppy drive into a hard drive. If you know what I mean."

Yoshi Kita beamed a smile. "Ah yes, Jaynus-san. Of course. You're an electronics man." Yoshi eyed the display. He gestured to a histogram analysis, color space and tiredness levels against Brady's digital image.

"Your fatigue levels show.."

Yoshi waved his hand across the screen to halt the Robot's speech.

"Your robot knows when I'm tired?" asked Brady.

Yoshi gestured them to walk. "Hai. It was developed originally by car manufacturers to sense a driver's fatigue. It analyzes a person's facial patterns, eyes, breathing, yawning."

"That's some clever shit." commented Jaynus.

"The nearest gentlemen's rest-room is four meters from you, Mr. Carter." said a robotic pillar.

Brady exchanged a look with Jaynus.

Yoshi halted them. "Apologies. I'm Yoshi Kita. Forgive me for not introducing myself."

"Joe Brady." Brady extended his hand as he looked around the place. He sighed.

Outside a Fashion-Health Doctors' Surgery, in Downtown Tokyo, a cop reeled off a stretch of DO NOT CROSS tape, sealing off an area. Fashion-Health places were sex establishments where clients could act out their wildest fantasies.

Seasoned Detective Inspector Edogawa removed his sunglasses. He placed his hands on his hips and eyed the street. He took in the sight of a CCTV camera and sighed at an Oshiro neon sign nearby. Edogawa had worked eight of the nine police squad divisions within The Criminal Investigation Bureau.

There was Controlled Substances or Organized Crime. There was the Burglary and kidnapping or blackmail Division. There was the division of bombs and explosives and there was a division for financial crimes, as well as two rapid reaction units.

Edogawa had not worked the cyber crime division. Edogawa's previous focus was the second division of robbery or sex-related crimes in Roppongi, a district of Minato, in Tokyo.

Roppongo meant 'six trees' and was popular for its nightclubs and hostess bars. It was a district that was home to many strip clubs and also the rich Roppongi Hills area.

Edogawa was tired of working in Roppongi. He had dealt with too many nightclub and bar owners, hotshot playboys, yakuza and dead hostesses, not to mention an influx of Nigerians, accused of spiking customers' drink in their own establishments.

One Nigerian man worked in a hostess bar and had fleeced a male customer's bank account of just over ten thousand dollars whilst he was drunk in a seedy bar.

Some would simply pickpocket them as soon as they were escorted into their bar by a hostess.

Many flooded their embassy and complained they were being racially discriminated against. It made police-work much more difficult, let alone more frustrating.

A colleague of Edogawa's told him he was angry by the hordes of alien minorities who had no will to adapt. "The Iranians in the nineties had their telephone card scams." his colleague moaned. "You had your South Americans and now it's the Nigerians!" he continued.

Crime was crime to Edogawa. It didn't bother him what nationality a criminal was. What he found amusing, however, was that many Nigerian criminals he came into contact with were actually quite easy to locate and track down for him.

Nigerian men sought marriage in order to obtain a visa, but that proved a much harder task for many.

Those he dealt with liked their women to be heavy-set and that type of woman wasn't too easy to find in Japan. "Find the chubby woman, find the criminal." Edogawa would grunt to his lower ranked colleagues.

The yakuza would also change their behaviors, too. They dealt heroin with the Africans.

Edogawa despised drugs. He once worked the case of a playboy hotshot who provided drugs to foreign hostess bar workers.

They were predominantly Australian and British girls, but there was the occasional Russian and European girl, too.

Edogawa thought he was onto the playboy, believing he was going to make a huge drug bust, however what he unearthed was much more alarming. He discovered seven severed, female heads, encased in concrete, with two more in the playboy's fridge.

The women, all hostesses, had been hooked on the playboy's drugs and of course wanted more.

He was actually disinterested in drugs or even making money from drug dealing. He had enough money. What he wanted was to simply dismember their bodies.

Poorer victims' families would often accept *mimaikin*, otherwise called blood money. It was condolence money, paid to the family for murdering their son or daughter.

Edogawa's current focus was homicide and unregistered weapons.

Some of the divisions often crossed over.

Edogawa did not know that every division would cross over that night.

"Inspector Edogawa?"

Edogawa turned to see his young protégé, Detective Rampo, step up.

Rampo flipped his notepad.

'Detective Rampo, what do we have?"

"An unidentified male. Yakuza. Two chest shots. One in the face." read Rampo.

"Witnesses?" asked Edogawa.

"Fashion-health sex worker. Nurse. Too distressed to make a complete statement. Just says a Westerner did it. Over and over."

"Westerner? Like Wild West Cowboy?" quizzed Edogawa.

It was like stepping inside an app.

An elegant, pretty Oshiro employee offered a glass of sparkling white wine to Jaynus.

"Our vineyards are located on the Island of Honshu." informed Yoshi.
Brady glances at Jaynus who smells the sparkling wine."

"Oshiro Champagne?" mocked Brady, declining a glass.

"How's your sparkling wine, Jaynus?" asked Yoshi.

"It's no Sugar Hill Beer, but I don't get offered those for free neither let alone in an elevator." Jaynus sipped his drink as the elevator ascended.

It was tech-geek porn as the elevator zoomed up the hi-tech shaft.

Jaynus gulped and put his glass on the tray.

Yoshi gestured for Jaynus look at the touchscreen. "Touchscreen. No buttons needed. Voice activated. Just say where you want to go."

"What I wanna go to the beach?" joked Jaynus.

"We have an indoor beach, Mr. Carter." Yoshi replied as if it was nothing.

"What?" Jaynus raised his eyebrows.

"We also have algae grown on fences wrapped around the building's exterior and turned into cosmetics."

"Algae?" breathed Brady.

"Algae is two-hundred percent better at absorbing CO2. It can cool a city down."

"Should wrap it around this guy." said Brady.

"That phone? Dial 1-800 Fuck You." Jaynus scowled.

"I thought the elevators were glass. See-through."

"Yeah, like Willy Wonka." said Jaynus.

"Willy what?" Brady frowned.

"Didn't you read to your kids?"

Yoshi touched the screen. "Sure you want an outside view?"

The Elevator walls became clear and depicted the true, high-up view. It overlooked the island.

The parking lot and its jungle-like outskirts.

Brady stepped back. He closed his eyes.

Masato and Philip stood by the bar in the Neon Bullet Hostess Bar.

It was evening and model hostesses, who couldn't dance for shit, swayed nearby.

Masato added creamer to his coffee.

The barman prepped cocktails for a hostess.

Frederick sat at the end of the bar. He lined toothpicks and squeezed ketchup into a bottle top. He eyed the bar and searched for something. "Jack Daniels."

"Double, straight, ice?" the barman asked.

"The bottle." demanded Frederick."

The barman frowned, and exchanged a look with Masato, who waves an 'OK', but occasionally watched Frederick, as he stood with Philip. "What's the old guy doing? He's freaking me out."

Frederick grabbed a packet of flour from the bar. He pinched a sprinkle of flour, dropping it into the bottle top. He poured a drop of Jack Daniels into it and started to gently mix it together with a toothpick. He snapped the end of the pick.

"What weapons do you have?" asked Masato.

"A few guns.. and my grandfather." replied Philip.

Frederick coated the end of a toothpick in the mix.

A Cooper Cooler wine-chilling device was housed on the bar.

Frederick was like a scientist. He rested a coated pick inside the neck of an empty wine bottle being speedy-chilled.

Mister White Headband sat in a corner, smiling and making a paper crane.

Frederick took the toothpick. He stepped over to Masato and grabbed a remote control, killing the music. Like a match, he struck the toothpick on the grooves of the remote control and ignited a flame.

Masato sighed and clapped twice. "Thirty years in jail and you learned how to make a matchstick."

"Wrong! A flamethrower!" boomed Frederick. He suddenly grabbed the coffee creamer bottle, flipped the cap and squeezed hard with his mega grip. He brought the flame to the ejected creamer powder.

WOOF! A jet of flame burst out!

Masato shielded himself.

Some of the girls reacted with a scream and a yelp.

Masato's arm was on fire. He padded himself down, damping out the flame.

Philip clapped. He was in absolute awe of his grandfather. "Bravo! Bravo!" Philip pulled a pack of E-cigarettes. He put it to his mouth.

Frederick dumped the creamer and grabbed Philip's wrist tight. "Smoke affects your night vision."

"Opa. It's an E-Cigarette." answered Philip, in German.

A motorcyclist stepped up to Masato, stepping in from outside.

Masato handed him an envelope. "Deliver this to Inspector Edogawa. Police Headquarters."

The motorcyclist nodded his head, turned and exited the bar.

"What now?" asked Masato.

Philip looked at him. "Wait for your corrupt police friends to hear about it by natural state of play. News will spread to the hundreds of violent groups around the city. Anger. Fear.

Terror. Unrest. Oshiro will be popular for being.. unpopular."

"The Kura Sasori Kai will be on the doorstep of Oshiro." said Masato.

Frederick stared his deep-set eyes at Masato. "Not just the doorstep, but.. Upstairs and downstairs and in my lady's chamber. There I met an old man, who wouldn't say his prayers, so I took him by his left leg and threw him down the stairs."

Masato frowned. "Are you talking about Brady?"

"Goosey-Goosey. The one who kills Brady will be considerably rich and have a seat at the table." continued Philip.

"What table?" Masato was confused.

Philip smirked

Frederick tried an E-Cigarette like a cigar.

There were more monitors inside the Control Room of the Oshiro Grand Plaza than the first day at Kindergarten. Screens depicted CCTV images of an indoor beach, a karaoke bar, a restaurant, the lobby, an onsen (spa) and Brady and Jaynus being led down a corridor within the building.

"Is he drunk?" asked Sarah Kita.

A young Oshiro security guard cum-tech-geek called Ringo jolted. He had just zoomed onto a Japanese woman in a bikini on the beach. He spun round in his chair, pushed up his dyed spiky hair. "Hmm?"

"Ringo Tanaka!" yelled Sarah. She was no longer a Brady. She was a Kita. "I said, is he drunk?"

Ringo tapped a touch pad. A body-scan of Brady appeared on his screen. "Scanning for toxins. Negative.

Sarah was pleasantly surprised. She thought for a moment and folded her arms.

Yoshi escorted Brady to a luxurious room. "This is your room, Joe. I forgot to give each of you a pin."

"Door code entry stuff?" Brady was tired.

Yoshi handed Brady and Jaynus a tiny pin badge. "We do not wish to confuse our guests with numbers. No offense."

"None taken. What's this for?"

"Your individual pin reacts to sensors around the building. Temperatures, lighting and scenery change according to you."

"Cool." Jaynus said.

"Kinda tracking my every move, huh? Like micro-chipping a dog?" Brady wasn't impressed.

"I wouldn't go as far to call you a dog, Joe, but I wouldn't want to lose you either. The pin can also open your room." Yoshi smiled, relaxing Brady.

"Sorry. I'm tired."

"I understand. I suggest our new massaging bathtub and a dose or pure oxygen. There are numerous health benefits of breathing oxygen-enriched air. It improves mental fitness and physical performance, riding headaches and fatigue. Also delays the aging process."

"Hell, I'll take a hit right now!" blurted Jaynus.

"We have an oxygen bar and free cans in every room. I strongly recommend it, especially before your commendation later."

"What?" Brady wasn't expecting it to be so soon.

"Yeah, I know. It's tomorrow."

"Ah, I see what has happened." realized Yoshi. "Time happened. Yoshi smiled.

Brady looked confused.

In his bathroom, Brady thumped the wall. He was angry. "Fucking time differences! Sonofabitch! Goddamnit!" it hit him. Time. They were ahead. He wasn't prepared, but then was he ever? He eyed his NYPD dress blues hung up behind him on the door.]

In an office within the Tokyo Metropolitan Police Department, Detective Rampo spoke with a couple of cops and reporters. "DNA comprising of blood and teeth identify the victim as Governor Honzo Kimura."

A uniformed cop approached and handed him an envelope. It was the same envelope Masato had given his motorcyclist.

Rampo eyed the envelope.

Detective Inspector Edogawa slept on a tatami mat in the sleeping facility of the Police Department.

The door opened and Rampo entered. He trod carefully, not to awaken any of the other sleeping cops. He crouched down to Edogawa and whispered into his ear. "Detective Inspector Edogawa?"

Edogawa opened one eye. He saw the envelope in Rampo's hand and sat up. He beckoned Rampo to open it.

Rampo opened the envelope. There was no note. Just an SD card, that fell into his palm.

Edogawa sat behind his desk, in his office.

Rampo closed the door.

"Close the blinds." Edogawa ordered.

Rampo did as he was told as Edogawa inserted the SD card.

The monitor depicted the nurse from the fashion-health club.

"That's the fashion-health nurse." Rampo stated the obvious.

"I see that. Just be quiet." told Edogawa as they continued to watch the footage, depicting the nurse, inside the clinical club.

She led Honzo Kimura into a room. She was the one who was electrocuted by Philip. She appeared normal, as normal as it was to be working in a club made to appear like a medical center. She was at home, in a familiar setting. This was her job. She gestured Kimura to sit down and told him to remove his shirt.

Kimura started to remove his shirt, which revealed his tattooed body. He barked at her, telling her to speak English.

The nurse popped a few buttons on her shirt, exposing her cleavage. She touched Kimura's chest and pouted at him. "Tattoos make your body cold." she said.

"Then you must warm me up." Kimura said, in broken English.

She smiled, turned and let her hair down.

Suddenly Brady entered. He had a gun in his right hand and fired twice. He shot Kimura in the chest!

The nurse screamed and crouched in a corner.

Brady towered above Kimura and shot him in the face!

The monitor flickered.

Brady tilted his head and lowered his gun.

The image froze on Brady's face.

Edogawa rolled his neck and stared at Brady's face on his monitor. "Here is our cowboy Westerner. Go. Printouts. Public Prosecutor.

Rampo opened the door and bumped into Ken, the cop who was being roughed up by Masato.

"Hey, Rampo, you coming out later?" Ken looked past Rampo and into the office. He fixed on the image of Brady on Edogawa's screen.

Edogawa noted Ken's look. He knew he had recognized Brady from that look on his face and waved him into his office.

Ken entered and closed the door.

8. [eight]

Dress Blues

There was a knock on Brady's door.

"Just a minute." he called out. Brady opened the door and was taken aback. He wasn't expecting his ex-wife Sarah to be stood there.

Sarah smiled. "You didn't RSVP."

Brady took a moment to speak. He was in awe of her glamor.

She neared sixty-years old and looked amazing.

Brady was dashing in his NYPD Dress Blues, adorned with medals. He exhaled. "Yeah, er, I sent it by snail mail."

Sarah passed him and entered the room, gazing around like she hadn't been inside there before. She had done so many times over. She had been behind practically every detail decision-making plan of that building. From soft furnishings to the cocktail drinks menu, she had authorized most.

"It's good to see you, Sarah."

She turned and looked him up and down. "It's good to see you, too, Joe."

It had been a long time since they last saw one another. Fifteen years? Maybe more.

She remembered more than he.

Brady had definitely lost count.

They embraced one another.

Sarah leaned in close to try and take in as much of his scent as possible, wondering if he smelt of booze and having a small part of her hoping that he did.

He didn't.

Not that day, but there were many days where he did.

AA didn't work out for Brady. In fact, on his first visit, he arrested two guys once they had left the building and started up their vehicles.

Both men protested their innocence and called Brady crazy, as well as other expletives.

He didn't care. It detracted him from the reason for his being there in the first place. Any excuse for a subject change.

"What's this bottle of whiskey doing in the sock drawer?" Sarah occasionally asked.

"Hey, Burt Lamb got a promotion." Brady would deflect.

"I thought he retired on ill health?" Sarah was suckered in.

"Have you been drinking?"

"It was George's birthday. The Captain said we could have a coupla drinks."

"Who's George?"

"George? You know. Maybe you don't. New kid. Nice guy."

"Well that's good to know." Sarah was suckered in once more and so Brady's game continued until she wasn't finally accepted it was indeed a problem and affecting every area of their professional and personal lives. She left him. Twice. Three times.

The fourth time was Brady's decision. He walked out. When he returned, Sarah was gone, leaving divorce papers on one broken chair because she had cleared everything else out.

A note simply read: All I have left you with is a broken chair because all you have left me with is a broken heart.

He was on his own. How could he function properly as an officer of the law?

Brady exhaled, holding her tight and breathing in as much of her scent as he could.

She smelt clean. Fresh. Brand new.

Brady thought hard, pressing himself for a memory of scents. What was that? Fabric softener? He would never have got it.

Sarah was wearing a Japanese brand. Parfum Satori, an independent perfume house in Tokyo. The fragrance was Nuage Rose to be precise and contained fruity pear and pink pepper with rose, jasmine and a hint of sandalwood. Sarah turned around and looked the Oshiro room over once more, despite knowing it inside out. She chose the room he would be staying in.

He discreetly checked her out. "You look.."

"Like a million dollars, I hope." interrupted Sarah.

"I was gonna say a million yen."

Sarah picked up an oxygen can from the bed. "You know that's about ten thousand bucks, right? – Don't get too hooked on these, by the way."

"Treated it like an asthma pump." he quipped, not really knowing what it was.

"Kids tell you about the divorce?" Sarah asked.

"Might have mentioned it. So, do you get to keep the fancy pants house in San Francisco?"

"So, nothing came about from seeing Connie, huh?" she quizzed him. It hurt her doing so, but she needed to know.

Connie was a former colleague from his days in the force. She got him through his worst days. Her and Bert Lamb, a colleague and dare he even have thought it, a friend, from when he was in the Academy, once picked him up in the gutter.

Brady was in such a drunken stupor he couldn't recall his own name let alone theirs. A lot happened that day. It was the day he met Jaynus. It was the last time he would hear his wife's voice, albeit on the phone and without a lawyer present and it was the day Connie expressed her affection for him. He was a wounded animal, physically and emotionally and required not just attention, but distraction. He had hurt her, too.

"No, nothing came about from seeing Connie. Jesus." he was edgy.

"Kids tell me everything, Joe."

"Got that right. Don't tell me shit."

"You never were the detective at home."

"Ah, I had my moments. So, what d'you get in the settlement? An airplane and a VCR?"

"Something like that." smiled Sarah.

Brady mumbled. "Knew you liked Japanese, but never that much."

Sarah chose to ignore his comment like she had done so many times over the years. "Well, it's my last hoorah with Oshiro today. - Thanks for coming, Joe."

He took it all in. He still loved her. He lowered his head and she faced him, looking him up and down.

Sarah straightened Brady's tie.

"I'm Sorry. For everything. I shoulda got a transfer."

"What, to Japan?" she scoffed.

"Yes, I woulda transferred to Japan."

"Joe, you can barely communicate in English. Do you honestly think you could handle Japanese?"

"Right now, I don't think I can handle anything Japanese." he said.

"We'll start with sushi and a speech. Let's go get your friend." said Sarah as she made out of the room

"Friend?" Brady thought about that for a moment. He remembered Jaynus and shook his head. 'What the hell am I doing here?' he thought to himself. "I guess so." he left the room and closed the door.

A beautiful digitized sky was present on the ceiling, along with an equally impressive golfing green and lake projected on the walls and flooring of the indoor golf simulator.

A tuxedo-clad Jaynus had just swung his wood, managing to get out of the bunker. He was impressed. He adored golf. 'Arms are made for swinging', he thought to himself. Whether it was a bat, a club or a racket, he loved to swing it. "I'm feeling a touch below par myself." he mused, nodding to another guest.

The guest turned to see Brady and Sarah watching.

Jaynus glanced round and did a double-take. "You scrub up well, Brady. Shit."

"You gonna be my date tonight? C'mon, time to go." smirked Brady.

"Domo arigato." said Jaynus to the guest, handing him his club. He stepped up to Brady and greeted Sarah with a smile.

She extended her hand to him. "Pleasure to meet you. I've heard a great deal."

"Yeah, all the bad fucking shit, too no doubt." Jaynus said, scowling at Brady. "I saw you on the TV. The flight over? Heard a lot about you, too over the years. Tried to get this asshole to call for a bunch of 'em."

"Yeah, so the kids said. Thanks for accompanying Joe all this way out here." Sarah said, genuinely.

"You are joking, right? A free flight, free accommodation, a crazy-ass indoor golf course and a bunch of futuristic electronics. This is heaven to me. Plus me going was part of the surgery bargaining deal. If you know what I mean?" Jaynus reeled off.

Sarah was pissed that she didn't know about Brady's ill health. She narrowed her eyes at him. "We'll talk about this later."

"What? Your building didn't detect it?" Brady sighed.

"It detects everything. It's like you, but faster and more polite."

Cameras flashed, bling sparkled and vehicles glistened outside the plaza.

Limousines, Rolls Royce, A Lexus or two and a handful of Bentleys pulled up. The occasional super-car powered in.

Valets took keys and Oshiro staff led glamorous guests in.

Old school businessmen, hotshots, rivals, honor and respect. They were all there.

Mei greeted guests in the lobby.

Their IDs flashed up on the screens, tripping various scanning imagery.

A groomed and bruised Masato entered.

A handful of press followed him.

"What happened to your face?" Mei was concerned.

"Your high profile guest. Listen, when I'm hurting, Oshiro shareholders hurt, too and so do the Kin Kaminari Kai." Masato blurted.

Mei was frowned, but she understood. She knew full well what he was saying.

In his beaten up old sedan, Edogawa drove across the bridge towards the island.

Detective Rampo was seated next to him.

"Important people tonight. For us Superintendents. For them, top Kin Kaminari Kai." Edogawa said as he drove whilst he fixed a tie.

"Is it true Governor Honzo was Kura Sasori Kai Godfather?"

"Yes." Edogawa grunted. He stared dead ahead, casting his eyes on the powerful looking structure of Oshiro Grand Plaza.

Rampo craned his neck and widened his eyes to see a holographic Oshiro logo rotating on top of the building. "Clever."

Edogawa wasn't impressed. He was more in awe when a reporter visited his home late at night to bring him ice cream in order to woo him into talking about a recent case he could do a story on. He smiled at the thought of receiving ice cream, but the thought went just as quick when the lights of the plaza closed in.

There was an aquarium in the function room of the Grand Plaza. It wrapped around the walls like a gigantic glass stripe.

Digital screens and tables. It was a full-on banquet as the guests were shown to their seats.

Members of the Kita clan exchanged bows and handshakes with fellow respectable Japanese businessmen and family members. They seated themselves down.

Jaynus pulled a box of dental floss and discreetly used it.

Brady shook his head upon seeing him to do.

Jaynus mouthed a 'what?'

Sarah put a comforting hand on Brady's. "Ready?"

He eyed Sarah, lovingly.

The massive fish tank was behind him.

He exhaled and stood.

Silence.

There were mostly Yakuza in the audience, but what did Brady know? Only that he was nervous.

He coughed and lowered his eyes to a crumpled piece of paper that was his speech. "Thirty years ago I was a young detective who got on a plane to meet a beautiful Oshiro Executive - and here I am again."

A handful of guests nodded and smiled. Some had headsets that translated his every word.

One old timer studied his Sharp Aquos cell phone. He looked horrified.

On the streets of Tokyo, a Bosozoku rides.

Six more bikes join along side. A biker gang in any other word.

"I can certainly say I'm older, but wiser, I don't think so." continued Brady.

On a street corner, a Yakuza biker was beating up a local stall owner.

The stall owner handed over some cash when the biker's cell phone sounded out.

The biker interrupted the bloody beating and looked at the message. He saw Brady's face, pictured with kanji.

The kanji simply read: AMERICAN GUEST AT OSHIRO MURDERS KURA SASORI KAI GODFATHER HONZO.

"Not a lot has changed since those days, except hair loss and insurance claims." said Brady in the function room.

Sarah smiled.

Jaynus tilted his head, knowingly.

In a tattoo studio, a naked man, on his back, was having a wabori tattoo on his back and butt by a guy who resembled the famous tattooist Horiyoshi the 3rd. He checked his email on an iPad type device to see Brady's CCTV image appear, alongside a dead Kimura.

"I didn't set out to be a hero that day.."

In an illegal gambling den, old Yakuza played baccarat. Televisions depicted sumo matches, horse racing and baseball.

Bodyguards played the slots.

A manager spoke to one of the guards, who subsequently whispered to his boss.

"I still don't consider myself to be one." stated Brady, continuing his speech.

On the Shuto Expressway, two hashiriya street racers were speeding along.

On the dash of one vehicle, a GPS display cut to Brady's image, accompanied by a 'WANTED for the murder of Governor Kimura' in kanji.

The car drifted round as if it was on ice.

A Sumo wrestler was thrown out of the ring and landed in front of a suit that looked up from a cellphone.

The suit whispered to the wrestler, who suddenly got up and walked out of the place, leaving everyone utterly confused.

Within the Tokyo Dome, the Big Egg Stadium, a Yomiuri Giants player was on the PITCHERS' MOUND.

A batter was the home plate and was about to swing when a suit casually walked over the diamond.

He spoke to him.

The bat dropped.

The suit and the batter then walked off.

"Takeshi Kida, about - who is this suited stranger on the field?" said the commentator.

Edogawa and Rampo flashed their badges to Oshiro staff outside the Grand Plaza and bowed to a doorman. Their Ids appeared at reception as they entered.

"Can I help you, Detectives?" said the robotic concierge.

Edogawa turned to the screen. He didn't think anything of it and simply held up his smartphone, which housed a picture of Brady's passport photo. "Where is this man?"

A humble Brady was in the middle of the room and received a medal from a Super Intendant General.

The room applauded him.

Sarah smiled proudly.

Jaynus clapped enthusiastically.

Brady smiled back. He quickly frowned when he saw Edogawa in a doorway and slotted his badge in his top pocket.

Edogawa whispered to a top police official who suddenly formed an extremely concerned expression.

US born President of Oshiro, James Kita was fifty years old. He sat with his three brothers, which included Yoshi and one sister.

Their ages ranged from thirty-two to fifty.

James Kita approached Brady to address both him and the audience. "I used to beg my father, Yoshinobu Kita, to tell me stories of the legendary Kintaro. Japanese folklore of a man-child, who fought monsters and demons. Kintaro didn't have many friends and those he did have were animal messengers. A reluctant hero, he was bossy and helped the weak. Now, my own children beg me to tell them heroic stories, though not of Kintaro, but of the legendary New York Detective Joe Brady. - Mr. Brady, in saving the lives of 136 Oshiro employees and preventing the theft of my family's fortune thirty-years ago. On behalf of the Kita family and the Oshiro Corporation. Thank you." James bowed.

The Kita family stood and bowed.

Brady was overwhelmed.

They shook hands when Edogawa suddenly handcuffed Brady!

Brady was completely taken aback.

Sarah and Jaynus frowned.

Sarah stood up.

"What's happenin' here?" Brady called out.

Guests began to mutter and point at Brady. Some scowled at him.

Sarah approached Brady. Concerned for him.

Jaynus stood up. He was baffled by the situation. "Jesus, Brady, what's going?"

"This man is being taken in for questioning." Edogawa commanded.

"He is a guest. How dare you embarrass us!" yelled James Kita.

"Inspector Edogawa?" whispered Detective Rampo.

The muttering became louder.

Guests were incredibly angry.

"He has murdered Honzo Kimura." announced one guest.

"The American has killed Governor Kimura." said another.

"The Godfather is dead." said others.

It was now a crowd instead of a formal event.

Brady found himself being led away, turning his head in every direction, trying to get a lock on Sarah, Jaynus and the entire situation.

James Kita was confused and saw several guests circle them.

"Am I hearing what I think I am?" said Sarah, understanding the Japanese mutterings within the room.

"What are they saying, Sarah?" yelled Brady. He was anxious and on edge.

Edogawa was tense, fully aware of the hostility and negative energy in the room. He knew full well he was about to open a can of worms.

Some guests pointed at Brady, angrily.

"He cannot go to the station?" insisted Detective Rampo.

Brady was stressed. He saw Jaynus pushing through.

"Why not?" asked Edogawa.

"Because there are hundreds of Kura Sasori Kai yakuza outside." continued Rampo, nervously.

"Please explain what's happening?" asked Sarah in Japanese.

"Who are you?" Edogawa asked. He turned back to Rampo. "What do the Kura Sasori Kai want?"

"To kill American, Brady-san." said Rampo.

Sarah was shocked. The words went through her body like an icy drill. She shivered.

Edogawa thought fast. He noted the angry guests around him.

It was like a courtroom gone wild.

He saw two Oshiro Guards and beckoned them over. "Do you have a secure holding?"

Some uniformed cops entered and took hold of Sarah, grippinhg her arm tightly.

Sarah winced with discomfort, eyeing the thin hand holding her arm.

Brady was led out of the room. "Sarah! Where are you taking me!"

"Joe! What have you done!" she cried.

"Nothing! I haven't done anything!"

"You must have done something! You always do something! Joe! Joe!"

"The fuck's going on, Brady?!" shouted Jaynus. He searched for them in the crowd, but soon lost sight of them. He was alone in a roomful of Japanese people and boy did he stand out.

Outside, three Oshiro Security Guards stood by the doors. They were wide-eyed and stared out beyond the forecourt.

Another guard exited and cockily joined them. "Heard you losers had a problem. Want me to help out?" he turned and saw the hundreds of bikers, black suited guys, low-level street thugs, cyber-punks and street racers before him. Armed with blades, bats with nails and guns. They were angry. They were all yakuza.

"Think you can help us losers now?" trembled one of the guards.

9. [nine]

Kataki-uchi

Brady was hustled into the elevator by Edogawa and an Oshiro guard.

James Kita followed them.

Brady wasn't too keen on much in life, especially elevators. "This how Japan treats all its guests?"

"Just the ones who are murderers." grunted Edogawa.

"What?" Brady was confused. He curled his lip and suddenly butted the Oshiro guard in the face. He swung his cuffed hands into the guy's gut, doubling him over.

James Kita tended to the controls.

Whoosh! The elevator ascended upwards at tremendous speed.

Skin on cheeks rippled.

"Joe, please cooperate."

Brady was about to kick off again.

Edogawa pulled a set of tiny needles and speedily jabbed one just below Brady's ear, then another behind his collarbone, temporarily paralyzing him.

Kita and Edogawa exchanged a look.

Brady worked his eyes around the elevator, unable to do anything else. He was fearful.

It wasn't long before Brady was dragged out of the elevator and to a much different part of the building.

Machinery and electronics were here, all behind glass panels.

Brady was dragged to a shiny square-shaped floor.

James Kita's retinas were scanned.

A panel opened.

Brady's police-issued cuffs were removed and bulky, futuristic-looking electronic ones replaced them. He jolted back and glanced at the cuffs. "Jesus. What the fuck was that?" Brady winced. He was alone when suddenly green laser beams jetted across, like bars. He was encased in a 'laser-cell'. He glanced around himself, then down at his cuffs and finally at Edogawa. "Who d'you think I am, Chewbacca?" he winced with pain and rolled his neck. Brady

"What's happened to him?" Edogawa spoke Japanese to Kita. He was as wary and confused as Brady when it came to the science fiction within the building. He just dealt with it better.

"You've been injected with a sedative and a tracking device." stated James Kita.

"Are you fucking crazy!?" blurted Brady.

Edogawa, James Kita and the Oshiro Guard look at him.

Sarah found herself pushed into another Oshiro holding facility

The room was a little different. Empty, even.

"You cannot do this! I am an Executive VP at Oshiro." she spoke in both Japanese and in English.

A cell-bed ejected from the wall, followed by a toilet and a sink. A partition rose from the floor.

Sarah was bemused. She hadn't known about this part of the building. She was frightened.

Outside was becoming more and more crammed as dozens upon dozens of Yakuza began to arrive.

Rampo was positioned in the lobby. He looked at the monitors and gulped. He exhaled, knowing full well this was the calm before the storm.

Edogawa eyed the green laser bars that secured Brady. He looked at him and nodded, grunting when he spoke. "I am Inspector Edogawa. Tokyo Metropolitan Police. Can you confirm you are Joseph Brady?"

"Yeah, I'm Joe Brady. Now get me the fuck out this.. iPhone."

"Joseph Brady, I am arresting you for the murder of Governor Honzo Kimura." continued Edogawa.

"Murder? I wanna call a lawyer now, dammit. Get me outta here!"

"There are no automatic Miranda Rights here in Japan. I can question you before you speak with a lawyer, Mr. Brady."

Brady was angry. He stepped forth, but singed his arms on one of the bars. He jolted back and looked at the Oshiro guard. "Hey, Nintendo? Open the jail."

"When arrested in Japan you will remain in jail until you are indicted or released." stated Edogawa.

Brady stared in disbelief.

Outside the Grand Plaza varied Yakuza started to approach the Oshiro guards, who stepped back, warily.

"Kura Sasori Kai business. Step aside." said a Bosozoku Yakuza.

One of the guards bravely straightened. "We have a special function. I cannot let you in."

Rampo was fearful as he saw the Oshiro guards slammed back into the doors outside.

The lobby was besieged by Yakuza.

Their criminal IDs flashed on walls and screens inside.

A cellphone vibrated and Edogawa takes a call. "Hai." Edogawa stepped away.

James Kita lowered.

Brady was becoming drowsy. He tried to fight the drugs inside him. "James. James, listen to me. I don't know what's going on here, but you gotta get me out."

Edogawa steps away. James Kita lowers.

Brady's drowsy.

"You've been arrested for murder."

"I've hardly been anywhere!"

"For both our sakes, it's best if we don't speak to each other."

"C'mon! What happened to the legend you tell your kids? Kintaro? What about all that?"

"Just a passionate line in a speech, Joe."

"Fuck you! How's that for passionate?" Brady yelled.

"Joe, please."

Brady smirked. He nodded his head and looked up. "So you failed, too, huh?"

"Excuse me?" James Kita frowned.

"Marrying Sarah."

"I'd rather not talk about it."

"I bet you don't. I always knew she was more into Oshi you than Oshi me."

"Let it go, Joe."

Edogawa lowered his cell and stepped up to James Kita. "There is a serious problem in the lobby."

"What kind of problem?"

"Hey! Hey! Speak English, damnit." yelled Brady.

"Kura Sasori Kai are inside." Edogawa said. He was gravely concerned and glanced at Brady He stepped to the bars. "Kataki uchi."

"Bless you?" Brady had no idea what Edogawa said.

"Anti-social forces. Violent groups. Kura Sasori Kai Yakuza are in the building, Mr. Brady. You killed their God-father. They now want to kill you. Kataki uchi. Blood revenge."

Brady was distressed. He looked at his cuffs and around the laser cell. He looked at the men. He was so confused. Tired. Drugged. "But I.. I didn't kill anybody!"

Edogawa, James Kita and a the Oshiro guard made for an elevator.

Sarah sat on the bed in her holding facility. She looked at the plain walls. "If you won't let me out, I'd like to have a nicer view!"

The walls suddenly changed to depict a Japanese garden, with cherry blossom.

Sarah tilted her head and stood up. "Call Ringo Tanaka."

Ringo stared at the monitors within the Control Room. He ate some potato chips and answered the call. "Ms. Kita. What have I done?"

"Put the potato chips down and listen for a minute."

"Ringo looked around the room, paranoid. He took in a brief glimpse of chaos on the monitors and slid the chips to one side. "It's pretty chaotic here."

"Can you track my location?" Sarah asked.

Ringo worked his touch-screen and frowned. "No. It just reads upper level."

"How about Joe? Can you locate him anywhere?"

"Tracking.. His pin tells me he's in his room."

Jaynus pressed himself, tight, against a wall in the lobby, dozens of Yakuza raced by.

Guards were overwhelmed and some are punched and kicked aside.

More Oshiro security guards appear. They're worried, both for their own safety and for the protection of the building itself.

Jaynus fixed on an elevator nearby. He stepped out and suddenly jolted when a motorcycle sped past him!

An Oshiro security guard addressed those around him on a digital loud speaker. "WE WOULD LIKE OUR GUESTS TO REMAIN CALM. IF IT IS SAFE TO DO SO, PLEASE RETURN TO YOUR ROOMS."

Jaynus made a dash through the crowds and to the elevator. "Excuse me. I said excuse me!" He shoved a thug

The thug slowly turned around and wielded a katana sword.

A light from the blade glistened across Jaynus' fearful face.

He saw the elevator doors swish open in the blade's reflection, just as the sword is brought down, slicing Jaynus' bow tie.

BAM! The thug was suddenly swiped away by a motorcycle.

Jaynus widened his eyes. "Shit."

The bike whipped round and entered the elevator with Jaynus.

Jaynus touched his throat and looked at his fingertips. There were specks of blood.

It was cramped inside.

Jaynus looked at the Bosozoku biker in the elevator with him.

"What? You prefer razors? Don't look at me like that. You're the one with a motorcycle in the elevator."

"Which floor would you like Mr. Carter?" asked the Robot Concierge.

"Huh? Where is Joe Brady?"

"Apologies, we are unable to locate the guest Joe Brady. How else can I help you?"

"Damnit, Brady."

"You..know.. Joe.. Brady"? mumbled the Bosozoku biker.

Jaynus frowned at the biker.

10. [ten]

Club Tropicana

It was equally chaotic at the Tokyo Police Department as it was at Oshiro.

Cops zipped this way and that.

The bruised cop Ken entered a locker room. He took a cellphone and watched fellow cops move like ants. "More police on the way, but also the Special Assault Team." he lowered the phone, discreetly.

In the function room, by the aquarium, Masato stood, cellphone in one hand, he poured himself a whisky with the other.

Concerned guests grouped together.

One old timer was being tended to. It looked like heart trouble.

Mei spotted Masato lapping it all up. She made her way over to him.

Masato smiled and wiped his mouth, lowering his whisky.

"What's your part in all of this?" asked Mei.

"D'you still have a room here?" Masato grinned.

Yoshi Kita walked approached them.

Masato sipped his drink again, but Yoshi swiped it from his hand.

"Kura Sasori Kai are everywhere!" Yoshi yelled.

"Father. Please." Mei pleaded.

"Masato." pressed Yoshi.

"They're here to get the American." Masato said.

"We have guests! A business!"

"Katagi ni meiwaku wo kakenai. Do not cause trouble to ordinary citizens. Isn't that the rule of thumb for us?" Masato gained more confidence as he stared at Yoshi.

Yoshi tightened his face. He Stared at the cocky Masato.

A SWAT Team helicopter neared the Oshiro Grand Plaza's roof as it travelled through the night, across the Tokyo skyline.

Brady swayed in his holding cell. He tried to stay focused. He looked at the elevator ahead. Suddenly, he leapt through the laser bars, like he was barging through a door. His left arm, leg and top of his head were singed. He looked at his cuffs and thought for a moment. Brady held his cuffs against a laser bar and burnt them off his wrists. Needle marks were seen on his wrist. Brady steadied himself and made for the elevator. He glanced around himself inside the elevator, trying to stay awake. "Whenever you're feeling powerless

Joe, remember that just one of your turds can shut down a whole swimming pool."

"Destination, swimming pool." came the robotic voice of the elevatior.

Brady curled his lip. "Huh?"

The Special Assault Team took up their positions upon the roof of the Grand Plaza.

On the ground floor, however, security guards speedily ushered guests out of fire exits.

A couple of Yakuza strode into a corridor and passed an open hotel room.

One of them stopped.

An attractive businesswoman was on her cellphone.

The Yak stared at her and licked his lips.

His comrade pulled him back. "We are are for the American, not to be rapists."

Jaynus ran down another corridor. He glanced around and pulled his tiny Oshiro phone.

The beautifully cool Club Tropicana pool sparkled.

The LCD ceiling depicted a starry sky, which glistened on the pool.

Brady rounded a stone corner and stopped. He stared.

Thirty Yakuza stood poolside.

Brady gathered his thoughts. He hadn't many actually. "How you guys doin'?"

They stared. Some had sunglasses, some had bizarre haircuts and some were slick and smart.

Brady's Oshiro phone sounded out. He frowned and retrieved it. "'Pardon me." Brady freakied out inside, as the raging Yakuza edged round.

They cocked their guns, pumped their shotguns and drew swords.

How the hell could he get out of that one?

The Yakuza were getting closer. They looked wild.

Jaynus yelled into his phone. He could see a Bosozoku biker revving up close behind, with a katana tight in his grip. "Brady Where you at?"

Brady exhaled into his phone. "Checking out the amenities."

"Well I'm about to have both my amenities cut off!"

"A lone Yakuza cockily made his way to Brady.

"Yeah. Can't talk right now, man. Just tell me this, are you safe?"

"No. When is anybody safe around you? You're a magnet to madness."

Brady pocketed the phone.

The Yakuza closed in and pulled a pair of nunchucks, when he suddenly slipped on the floor. He landed with an almighty crack! His neck snapped and he died in a twisted heap on the brilliant white tiles.

Brady squatted down to his level and chuckled. "That right there is a personal injury claim. No wet floor sign." He picked up the nunchucks. "Should call Yakuza Lawyers 4U. Now what am I supposed to do with this? Put up a shower curtain?" Brady waved the chucks like a gym ribbon. He looked up to see the Yaks looking angrier. His grave face said it all until he fixed on a grenade on the dead Yakuza's waistband.

The dozens of Yakuza started to scream as they suddenly advanced for Brady.

Two appeared behind him.

Bullets were fired, breaking up the tiles.

There was nowhere for him to go. Brady grabbed the grenade and took cover.

Water was pierced.

Brady eyed the pool. Wide-eyed, he pulled the pin to the grenade and threw it into the water.

Plop.

The grenade slowly sank to the bottom of the pool.

"Time to die, American."

"You know I'm a V.I.P here, right?" he looked to a wall and double-took at a 'NO BOMBING' sign.

The grenade exploded. Like lightning underwater.

A bubble surfaced and then a BOOM!

The bottom of the pool cracked.

Water jetted upwards.

In one of the Beni Hana type Oshiro restaurants, the ceiling cracked. Like an earthquake, cracks zig-zagged

A water drop fell onto a hotplate and sizzled.

The chef looked up and frowned.

A drop fell into a wine glass where a hot couple sat, unaware of the chaos occurring elsewhere.

They looked up when the ceiling suddenly crumbled and water started to gush in.

Diners and staff began to flee. Most of them were washed away by the sheer force of water.

Jaynus was still being pursued by the Bosozoku biker.

He ripped his throttle back and formed a crazy-eyed look.

Jaynus rounded a corner and into another corridor. He was extremely fearful and hesitant at what to do next. He saw a pillar on one side. He glanced to the other side of the corridor and saw a statue in a doorway.

The sound of the bike became louder and louder.

Jaynus pushed the pillar over. He did the same with the statue and quickly dodged the oncoming biker, who raised his sword and let out a battle cry.

The bike connected with the toppled pillar an statue and the biker crashed into them.

The rider fell from the bike and rolled, dropping his sword.

Jaynus stepped over and kicked him. He kicked again, but the biker rolled over and despite being in a bad way and on his side, he kicked the shit out of Jaynus.

Jaynus winced with pain, clutching his ribs and crawled to a wall. He felt something in his pocket and frowned. He removed his pack of dental floss and then saw the rotating back wheel of the bike. Jaynus suddenly reeled off a length of floss and wrapped it around the biker's neck. Jaynus struggled.

The Bosozoku biker grabbed Jaynus' leg, but Jaynus managed to weave the pack of floss into the back wheel. He then ripped back the throttle.

The bike twisted this way and that.

The wheel span like crazy and in no time at all the Bosozoku biker was garroted by the floss.

The bike smashed into a digital painting in the corridor. Jaynus shielded himself and cringed at the bloody mess. He noted the katana samurai sword on the floor, glistening nearby.

Brady eyed the water that swirled down a hole, which he just created.

Yakuza closed in. Their faces mean and out for the kill.

Brady leapt into the swirling water. He was sucked down, into a plughole of a giant sink.

Bullets fired into the pool.

Some yakuza staggered and fell in. Some decided to jump in after Brady.

Water continued to pour into the restaurant.

Brady fell down from above. He landed awkwardly. Painfully. He was wet, drowsy and wired.

An extraction fan creaked.

Brady widened his eyes. He rolled as the fan crashed to the floor! Brady gasped. He eyed up his new surroundings.

There was less water pouring in, but enough on the floor and dripping all around.

Brady got to his feet. He wiped his face when a hand reached out of the water and grabbed his leg, pulling him down into the water. Brady punched the yakuza in the face. He jabbed again. "Think you're a fucking anaconda?" he turned and saw another yakuza surface from the water. "What is this? Yakuza Sea World?"

The Yak lunged at Brady, who caught his fist.

Brady pulled the yakuza into a row of hanging pots and pans.

His head clanged and bonged with each pot sounding out what Brady thought were the first seven bars of 'Ode to joy'.

Brady frowned. He received an elbow to the nose.

The yakuza delivered a two-punch combination to Brady's face and grabbed his neck, squeezing tight.

Brady was forced back. He was weakened. His eyes rolled.

A drip hit the hot plate and fizzed.

Brady managed to grasp the Yakuza's hair and he pulled his face down to the hot plate.

The yakuza's face sizzled and fried. The yakuza dropped.

Brady exhaled and rubbed his neck. He slowly looked up to see a Sumo wrestler, in a booth, with a large amount of food in front of him.

The Sumo turned. Got up and bound for Brady. In an instant he was bear-hugging him tight, squeezing the life out of him.

Brady managed to work and arm out from under the stinky, sweaty armpit. He pulled chopstick from the Sumo's hair and rammed it into his ear!

The Sumo suddenly released Brady and dropped down dead into the water.

Brady breathed out. He rested against a work surface and saw the burnt face of the yakuza nearby. He painfully removed his NYPD Dress Blues jacket and flung it over the yak's face. He was in agony. He wiped his bloody face with water and exhaled.

Jaynus was also in pain. He gripped his newly acquired katana and admired it. He liked it. He twirled it round, but it cut his thigh. "Motherfucker! Ugh! Shit!" he staggered to a booth in a wall. "Ow. Jesus Christ."

Images of Jesus suddenly appeared on a digital wall, accompanied by various texts.

The booth spoke. "Jesus Christ. Also known as Jesus of Nazareth." The images and voice stopped.

Jaynus eyed his cut leg.

"What would you like to know?" asked the Oshiro booth.

"Jaynus looked at the sword. He tightened his grip. "I wanna know how to use this sword without cutting off my damn leg."

A live digital image of Jaynus with his sword appeared in front of him. The image was captured and minimized. A grid covered the image.

"Jaynus Carter, you have requested information on how to use a Katana. A traditionally crafted Japanese sword. Originally worn by the Samurai in feudal Japan."

Jaynus was impressed and sought to learn more.

11. [eleven]

3D

At the Kanda Shrine in Tokyo, Frederick and his grandson Philip walk under the two story gated entrance.

The bright vermillion along with the hundreds of paper lanterns illuminated the courtyard.

Frederick stopped. He was a towering figure between stone lion-dogs.

Mister White Headband followed several steps behind, like a servant.

Philip checked his Smartphone with an earpiece. "Local news reports Yakuza disturbances at Oshiro."

"Put away your technology." requested Frederick

"It's technology that is enabling us our path of destruction, Opa."

"Maybe so, but technology has also been the cause of why we're here in the first place. You need to learn the truth. The reason behind it."

"I don't understand. Behind what?" Philip was confused. He adored his grandfather, but believed his yeas of being incarcerated had ruined his mind.

Frederick made for the steps of the shrine.

At the chozubachi water basin, Frederick took the wooden dipper with his right hand. He filled it with water and poured it over his left hand. He then took the dipper in his left and poured water over his right. Frederick poured water into his cupped left hand. He rinsed his mouth with that water and then spat it back out into the palm of his hand. Frederick pulled a handkerchief. He dried his hand.

Philip watched his grandfather closely.

Frederick climbed the stair. He tossed a coin into the sasenbako offerings box. He rang the suzu bell twice and stepped back. He bowed twice and then clapped twice. Frederick spent a few moments in prayer.

Philip watched him.

The elderly Mister White Headband watched Frederick proudly and occasionally nodded.

Frederick straightened. He descended the stairs.

Philip stared. "How do you know what to do? Opa, have you been to Japan before?"

"Our family have always gone to Japan. It's where it all started."

Philip shook his head. He was more confused than ever. "You're going to have to explain to me because I think prison made you lose more than just thirty years."

"No, you've missed over one hundred and fifty years!"

"But, what about Brady?" asked Philip.

Joe Brady is just a fly in the ointment. Oshiro, the Kita clan, they are our family's enemy. *They* betrayed us."

"But.. My father, my uncle." Philip was becoming frustrated.

"My sons. They tried to take back what was rightfully theirs."

Philip scowled. He was in total disbelief. He exited the shrine and downed the steps, followed by Frederick. "No. It was Brady. He killed.."

"And his action subsequently led to my imprisonment? An action leads to a reaction. Listen. There was always Oshiro. Always Kita. They stole from us first. Understand this." Frederick insisted.

Philip tried to take it in whatever 'it' was.

Thirty armed yakuza pushed their way inside the lobby of the Oshiro Grand Plaza.

Various staff darted around.

Fearful cops and security didn't know what to do.

A uniformed cop out-stretched his arms by an elevator as Yaks approached.

"Stop! I will be forced to shoot!"

"Cops are too scared to use guns."

The cop's hand trembled over his gun.

The impatient Yakuza shot the officer in cold blood!

Panic unfolded.

Angry cops pulled guns and unleashed a hail of bullets.

A gunfight occurred in the lobby as yakuza fled and entered elevators.

Some returned fire.

More yakuza piled inside.

It was bedlam.

SWAT members descended a stairwell. Their guns trained. Their form was tight.

Ringo had been joined by Edogawa and James Kita in the Control Room. They watched the monitors which depicted the chaos within the Plaza.

Cops and guards were chased, sliced and shot as they fled the various Yakuza.

The exploded swimming pool of Club Tropicana was seen.

Edogawa pointed at the pool. "What is below the swimming pool?"

"A restaurant." Ringo replied.

Edogawa turned to see Yoshi Kita, Masato and Mei enter the control room. "Show me the restaurant."

Ringo is frustrated. He shook his head.

Masato eyed the pool.

"Main camera's out." Ringo said.

"Look at the pool!" cried Masato.

"Is this the work of Kura Sasori Kai?" asked Yoshi, angrily.

"No, brother. This is the work of Joe Brady." Said James Kita.

Yoshi became enraged. "I thought he was imprisoned!"

"I guess he must have escaped." said James Kita.

"First he murders Kimura, then he murders the business."

"Arrested for murder. Not charged." corrected Edogawa.

"Video evidence like that, only a matter of time." Masato said.

"How has he murdered the business?" quizzed Yoshi.

"A murdered Godfather and avenging yakuza is an unpopular business." Masato shrugged.

Edogawa watched Masato.

Mei did, too.

"Where is Sarah Kita?" asked Yoshi.

James glanced at Ringo and then Edogawa. "Oshiro Hospitality."

"James, we need to talk business." insisted Yoshi. "Inspector Edogawa, excuse us." Yoshi gestured Mei to walk, then James. Masato followed.

"Masato? How did you know it was video evidence?" Edogawa asked.

Masato stopped. He thought for a moment and grinned at Edogawa. "This is Tokyo. You're always on video." Masato gestured to a dome camera above Edogawa.

He looked up, then back to Masato, but he and the Kitas had left the room. "Who is watching us on this?"

"Senior Security. Yes! I've an active restaurant cam." Ringo brought a view of the flooded restaurant. He worked a stick to look

Destruction. Water.

Bodies.

Brady. He ate a stick of grilled chicken and leaned against a work surface. Water seeped out a gaping hole above. "Gotchaselves an indoor waterfall." His Oshiro phone sounded out.

'Jaynus Carter is calling you'.

Brady took out the phone and noticed the pins in his elbow. He cringed at the sight of them. "Jesus. Jaynus. You OK?"

"Not really. You?" replied Jaynus on the other end.

"Ha. No. Was just flushed down a giant lavatory."

Jaynys gripped his sword and his phone. He wore a traditional hachimaki headband as he stood in an empty bar.

The lights flickered. "You finally caught up with your shitty life, right?"

"Something like that. Listen. I don't know how, but we need to find a cop."

"I've seen a few dead ones."

"No. This guy's a detective. An Inspector Eddo something." Brady trudged through the water, out of the restaurant.

"And if I find Inspector Eddo?"

"He must have the evidence on me."

"Waitaminute. Evidence on you for what?" Jaynus shrieked.

Brady painfully rested against a doorway, like a cowboy. "I didn't tell you? Funny. Guess I was pushed for time. You know, between being holed up in a game of laser-tag to a yakuza water-slide."

"What fucking evidence, Brady?"

"Uh, murder. Pretty much murder."

Jaynus was in disbelief.

Lights sparked.

Electrical short circuit.

Several party go-ers appeared.

Jaynus jolted and swiped his sword like a pro. He swiped again and again. He cut through nothing.

The people were holographic images.

"Hey? Jaynus? Can you hear me?" Brady's voice sounded out.

"Yeah. I hear you. Things just got a little Tupac Coachella." Jaynus chirped.

"What?"

"Don't worry." Jaynus chuckled. "So, who d'you kill?"

"Apparently that guy. Governor Honzo Kimura."

"Damn right, cos it looks like murder. Plus you have a motive, idiot."

"I know!" Brady was flustered.

"You even saw him in the street!" Jaynus added.

"Alright, dammit. Look." Brady stopped. He saw the hashiriya street racer further down the corridor.

He was angry and stared at Brady, who straightened. He dangled a chain and motioned slicing Brady's throat with his finger.

Brady clenched his fist. To him, the racer was just another pain in the ass itch that he just needed to scratch.

"You there, Brady?" asked Jaynus.

"I gotta go. Find that detective." barked Brady. He pocketed the phone and entered the corridor. "OK, bone-head, how d'you wanna play this?" Brady locked eyes with the man. A twinkle caught his attention and he turned.

It was a Christmas tree. It was a real one, too and not some holographic image or digital screen.

Brady, in an instant, grabbed the tree and started to charge, insanely, at the street racer.

The street racer widened his eyes with disbelief as Brady paced towards him, Christmas tree in his grip, like a knight about to joust.

Suddenly the top of the tree had made contact with the street racer's body, piercing right through him.

"Ugh! Merry fuckin' Christmas!" Brady screamed as he stumbled back and took in the cringe-worthy sight of the street racer.

A bauble fell off the tree and rolled on the floor.

Brady exhaled, turned and took a step away. He glanced back round and stopped in his stride.

A second street racer stepped up, then ten more yakuza.

Brady swallowed. He should have known by now that things never went according to plan.

In the Oshiro Control Room, Edogawa gestured to live CCTV of Jaynus in the bar.

"Jaynus Carter." Ringo stated.

Edogawa ordered him to bring Jaynus to the Control Room.

Sarah tapped a digital tablet whilst sitting within the holding facility. She jolted when she saw James Kita staring at her.

"You cannot override the system." he said.

Sarah was angry. She saw Yoshi stood next to him. "James, darling. Update me. What's going on here?"

"Tosho reports shares are falling." James was serious.

"I'm not asking for a stock exchange status. I'm Executive Vice President of Marketing, not the VP of Finance. I'm trying to get my head around why we have it anyway but get me out of this very peculiar holding facility, so I can help out." Sarah barked.

"That's not going to happen, Ms. Kita." said Yoshi.

"Ms. Kita? Excuse me, but I have been an integral part in shaping and branding this company into what it is today. Don't you forget that!" Sarah narrowed her eyes at Yoshi.

"And don't you forget that the person who is ruining the business is your ex husband." replied Yoshi.

"No. My ex husband is *your* brother. My ex ex is Joe." corrected Sarah.

James took a call. He hung up and eyed a pissed Yoshi. "We've been infiltrated by the Kura Sasori Kai." James said in Japanese.

"James. Yoshi. Listen. I've worked for Oshiro for 35 years. I was married to a Kita for five years. Did it ever occur to you that during one of those days I might just work out what was going on? Seeing that there is a large amount of diverse, highly suspicious activity occurring here in this company on a daily basis? I know your enemy is the Kura Sasori Kai, The Black Scorpion Association. I know Oshiro, the Kita Clan is Kin Kaminari Kai, The Golden Thunder Association. Yakuza. Gokudo. Something a former husband, Joe Brady is definitely not a part of." Sarah sent a mean-ass stare at the brothers.

Yoshi bowed his head. "Sarah, forgive me. Us. What would you advise?"

"I'd advise to lock yourselves away like you've done here with me. Maybe go to technology and get some bulletproof vests and.. I tell you this; if there's a bad guy, Joe will find them. He will work out why they're here and he will probably kill them, too."

Frederick looked out onto the city of Tokyo from the Observation Deck of City Hall. He diverts his attention to a television screen.

The screen depicted a commercial.

The Indian Ocean was shown.

A yacht was seen.

A voice-over sounded out over the images. "In the Indian Ocean, paradise is disturbed."

Somali men, with AK47s and RPGs bumped the waves in a speedboat.

"Young Somali men, with no economic alternative than to hijack and sometimes rape and kill." the voice belonged to an arrogant television reporter called Robert 'Bob' O'Mally. Robert O'Mall was a Larry King type. He had risen the regionals to primetime in a speedy fashion, though mostly due to dirty, cheap journalist tricks. Bob exposed Brady as a cop during the Oshiro siege. The report nearly cost Brady his life.

The Brady family had a bitter taste in their mouths whenever O'Mally's name was mentioned, let alone when he was seen on TV.

"Off the southern coast of Somalia, a key anti-piracy operating base has more than 200 suspected pirates in their custody. I talk to the one who kidnapped me for nine days." O'Mally stood, with a serious expression, in the surf of an Indian shore.

A graphic of a naked O'Mally against the US flag and the words "ROBERT O'MALLY: STARS & STRIPPED" appeared on screen.

Another voice over kicked in. "Catch Robert O'Mally Stars & Stripped only on Fox."

Frederick nodded. He turned to Philip, who toyed with a smart phone.

"Where's the original data of the murder?" Frederick asked.

"It's all on here." Philip waved his own phone.

"So what you're telling me is the evidence that could release Brady from custody is stored on your handy? Your mobile phone?" Frederick was bemused.

"Jah."

"Are you insane?!" Frederick blurted in Japanese. He slapped Philip around his face.

Philip became tearful.

"You complete fool. Do you not think somebody could retrieve the data?"

"Not Brady." Philip replied.

"Brady's a resourceful man. If scientific hooligans can hack Marconi's Wireless Telegraph in nineteen hundred and three, they can hack a cellular phone over a hundred years later. We need to go to Oshiro."

"No."

"Yes." Frederick stared at his grandson.

Bullets tore into the walls of a corridor, deep within the Oshiro Grand Plaza.

Members of the yakuza were in a full-scale gunfight with a highly elite SWAT team.

A member of SWAT was riddled with bullets. His body armor was ripped and torn. The force lifted him off his feet. He landed in a bloody heap.

A Yakuza delivered a crazy, animalistic roar, as he gripped his two machine pistols. He felt truly victorious that he had felled a man of law and order.

In no time at all, the remaining SWAT members exacted their revenge on the yakuza who had killed their colleague.

The yakuza was practically split in half from being shot by a Remington 870 pump action shot gun.

Gun smoke and plaster dust clouds covered the bloodied walls and shot bodies strewn across the corridor. It was sheer carnage.

Ringo turned and smiled at Edogawa. "Security is bringing him up."

Suddenly Masato entered the room and shot Ringo in the head.

Blood and brain spattered across Ringo's workstation and monitor.

Edogawa pulled his gun, but was hit in his arm. He staggered behind a desk though managed to pull his trigger twice, shooting Masato in his gut.

Masato dropped to his knees, letting go of his gun. Blood seeped from his mouth. He was in complete and utter disbelief. He couldn't believe that he had been shot

Edogawa stepped out from behind the desk and soon towered above Masato, who gargled blood. "Who else wants the American dead?" he said in his native tongue.

Masato smiled a blood-toothed grin. "Mueller-san." he flicked a knife and stabbed the blade into Edogawa's thigh.

Edogawa grabbed Masato's knife-hand, forcing it onto itself.

Masato choked on his blood and died within seconds.

Two Oshiro guards entered the room, widening their eyes with shock.

Edogawa released his hold on Masato's hand letting him slump to the flood. He looked up at the two guards, horrified before him.

Jaynus stood behind them and took in the scene. "The guards said I was being taken to the control center, but it looks to me like there ain't too much control going on." he eyed the dead Masato on the floor and then Ringo, bloodied in the office chair, still at his workstation. Jaynus eyed up at Edogawa and raised his eyebrows.

Brady took in his surrounds. He was stood in an open-plan office. He glanced around, frantically and decided to continue his pace.

A partition suddenly ejected from the floor.

Brady jogged into the newly presented wall and ended up on his back. He winced. "Jesus." Brady stared upwards as the room changed and a computerized voice sounded out.

"Smart tech activated. Please remain still as we conserve energy and office space for one." The ceiling lowered, the temperature changed and walls moved. A workstation for one appeared around a pained Brady.

"Fucking Edgar Allan Poe Matrix bullshit." Brady caught sight of eleven Yakuza entering the moving space. He saw a door, rolled over to get to his feet and made for it. He weaved and smashed through partitions, as outsmarted Yakuza tripped and stumbled, trying to pursue him.

Some fired their guns, splitting and puncturing new walls as Brady fled.

Brady entered a print room.

There wasn't much in there at all; just a handful of plastic sculptures and innovative buildings and structures. There was, however, a large 3D printer.

Brady curled his lip and breathed heavy. He was trapped inside a small room whose sole purpose was to house a printer. Beyond the door were eleven bloodthirsty yakuza.

They wanted Brady dead, believing he had killed their Godfather.

Edogawa had his wound tended to by a guard.

Another guard rested Ringo elsewhere and covered his face, respectfully.

Jaynus eyeballed footage of Brady killing Kimura. He couldn't get his head round what he was watching.

The hell bent yakuza neared the print room. Some had got wise of the various partitions that popped up every so often, adjusting to the energies and space within the room.

Brady, meanwhile, was wired and began to kick the shit out of a sensor, simultaneously talking on his Oshiro cellphone. He had called Jaynus and believed well and truly that his time had come. He really didn't want to die in a print room.

The yakuza closed in on the room. They were wary of the partitions.

"Damnit, Jaynus!"

"Don't damnit me, Brady. I've just seen video of you kill Governor Kimura in cold blood."

"It wasn't me!"

"Are you sure you didn't accidentally whack a yak?" Jaynus quipped.

"No! Look, whatever you saw, it wasn't me."

The print room door shook as it was kicked, then shot from outside.

"You alright? Where are you?" Jaynus asked.

"In a Rubik's Cube. Can you get a tech guy to help me out here?" Brady was nervous. He had backed himself into a corner.

"Apparently, the best one available is now dead." Jaynus said as he eyed up Ringo's corpse.

"Shit! Fuck! OK. Get an outside line and call Daniel Simmons. D'you hear me? Dan Simmons."

"How! How'd I get hold of him?"

"Eve will know. Call Eve!" Brady barked.

Yakuza gathered. Some were quite bemused by the auto-shifting office.

12. [twelve]

Eve Brady

The Trader Joes store, in New York City, was open and Eve Brady read a cereal box in one of the aisles. Eve was in her late twenties and heavily pregnant. She was the only daughter of Sarah Kita and Joe Brady. Just like them both, she had fight in her. Eve studied medicine and dentistry at Rutgers University.

Her father would joke that when she graduated, her dentistry skills would help him a great deal in gaining a confession from a scumbag or two.

There was a period of time when Eve didn't see or speak with her father. It was after she graduated and she took off without telling a soul where she was going.

Naturally, Brady tracked her down. He discovered she had got work as a cabaret dancer on board a cruise ship, sailing around the Caribbean. As good or bad luck would have it, Brady had been asked to represent the New

York Police Department in Trinidad and called in a few favors, enabling him and his colleagues to get on the same ship instead of flying direct.

Unfortunately for everybody on board, especially the Bradys, untoward forces were also at work.

Eve was frightened and put her life in the hands of her heroic father. As scared as she was, Eve knew she was safe with him. She wanted so much to forget about the traumatic experience, but it was as vivid to her then as it was the day it took place. She vowed never to go on a boat again. She didn't want to remember. That was a story for another time.

Brady preferred for her not to dance in front of him again.

"You can even turn paradise to shit!" Jaynus mocked Brady when learning of the disastrous overseas trip. It was a tale he would tell another time.

Eve raised her cellphone to her ear and continued to read the cereal box. "If you're gonna ask me about Personal Protection Insurance, I'm not interested. Thank you."

"In a funny kinda way, I am." Jaynus joked.

"Jaynus Carter?"

"Yeah, that's right." Jaynus replied.

"Why are you working in a call center? I thought you were in Japan with my Dad." Eve said, curiously.

"I am in Japan. It's why I'm calling. Your father's asked to get in touch with Dan Simmons. It's pretty damn important."

Eve dumped the cereal box into the cart and pushed it up the aisle. "I don't have any idea where he is and we're not exactly on speaking terms. Dad'll have to find another way to reach him."

"That can't happen."

Eve stopped. She became panicky and started to breathe heavy and fanned herself. "What's wrong? Is my father OK?"

"Is he ever OK? Look, if you know a way to get to him, that'd be super-cool. Maybe your brother would.."

Eve interrupted. "No. Definitely not. He wants to kick his ass, too. Alright, um, I know who could help. Give me your number and I'll get them to call you."

The letters 'E.W.P.I.' glistened on the door.

The over-tanned secretary retrieved her telephone in her Miami office. "E.W.P.I. How may I help you? Oh, hey you. He's out on a job, but I could try him." she looked to a closed door and a name etched on the frosted glass window: ED WILLIAMS PRIVATE INVESTIGATOR. A sunny palm tree beach scene reflected on the glass.

A pink Cadillac cruised along Ocean Drive.

African American Ed Williams sat comfortably behind the wheel. The former Los Angeles cop, in his Panama hat and shades, beamed a smile and spoke on his hands-free phone. "Baby girl! Eve Brady! What can I do for you today?" Ed was such a happy soul. Serious when he needed to be, but he absolutely, utterly loved life. He had met Brady thirty years ago during the Oshiro mall siege.

His superiors believed Brady to be one of the terrorists, but Ed Williams knew deep down that he wasn't. In fact, Ed believed Brady was a cop from the outset and so assisted him from afar as Brady reluctantly battled the bad guys and saved the day. Ed stayed on as a police officer for several more years, but as his family grew, so did his paperwork. He didn't want his kids growing up in LA. He also didn't want to miss his kids growing up, period, so decided to set up his own detective agency in Florida. He made the right decision.

The loving smile on his Ed's wife's face reminds him of that every day.

"Uncle Ed, am I disturbing you?" asked Eve.

"Not at all. Just out on my morning run. How can I help?"

"It's for my Dad, actually."

Ed had concern mixed with his chuckle. "Oh, here we go. I'm listening."

Eve Brady chomped a carrot stick and dipped it in humus as she talked. "One of his not-friends is with him in Japan and they're both in a bit of shit."

Ed pulled his car over. "Sounds about right. Go on."

"I'm very Sigourney Weaver right now and I need to find the father of my soon to burst out of me Alien."

"So Joe can kick his butt?" smirked Ed.

"Surprisingly no. I think it's more important than that."

"Whoa. Hold on, Cowgirl. More important than your first-born? I'm sensing.."

Eve cut in. "Please. Don't say it."

"OK. Give me the name of the baby-daddy. I presume that it's Daniel."

"Yes it's Daniel's!" Eve blurted.

"It's Simmons, right? Last known location? Any idea at all?"

A video games convention took place in the Philippines.

Daniel Simmons shifted gears like RoboCop in a racing car simulator. He finished the race in first position and punched the air. "Yes!" Dan was all-things computer. He was everything Brady was not. He was digital and modern. He had been a hacker and probably still was in some form or other. A Royal pain in the ass to corporations and the System. He became a vlogger and gained himself a huge internet following. School kids would watch him play the latest video games and his geek cred would rise dramatically. He became a Youtube sensation.

"Kids watch you play video games?" Brady would say.

"Yeah."

"And you get paid for that?"

"Yeah."

"Why don't kids play their own games?" Brady once asked.

"They do, but I'm showing them how to do it."

"Let 'em figure it out for themselves."
Brady didn't get it.

In a bizarre twist of fate, several years
prior, Brady had somehow stumbled into Dan
Simmons' nerdy world.

Dan had pissed off a nasty bunch of
cyber terrorists by not following their exact
instruction. He had somehow managed to work
his way into Brady's life and before he knew it,
he was dating his daughter, Eve.

Brady, a few years down the line,
eventually, accepted his daughter's relationship
with Daniel Simmons, trying to convince
himself that it was Eve's good nature and her
caring for a potentially autistic young man with
special needs, than just her simple love for him.
However, when Eve fell pregnant and Dan
couldn't handle it and went missing, Brady, as
well as his son, blew a fuse.

Knowing this would happen just
propelled Dan further. "Like the best game
ever. Like ever." Dan said to himself.

Brady eyed the ceiling and then the
walls of the print room. There was no escaping
this room, except via the way he entered it.

The blade of a fire axe slammed through
the door.

Brady pressed himself into the corner
and swallowed.

Dan Simmons weaved through the
crowds of the video game convention. He
passed a host of peculiarly dressed characters.

Cosplay folk.

Scantily clad women in medieval looking outfits growled at him as he walked. They occasionally jabbed a spear or a far-too realistic short sword towards his face.

"Whoa! Jesus!" he gasped. He checked some hot Filipino babes and smiled at them.

One lowered her top and pushed her breasts together, forming one hell of a cleavage.

Dan stopped and stared at her. He frowned when she winked at him, then noticed a man stood behind with a radio control device.

He was controlling her!

The woman wasn't even real.

"You gotta be kidding be. An RC woman? That's something I have to get." he muttered.

Suddenly, a beefcake security guard blocked his path. He was enormous.

"Jeez. Your arms are bigger than my waist." Dan said, gently touching the beefcake's left forearm. "So realistic. What is that? Some kind of expensive latex?" his eyes searched for someone behind.

"Not latex. Real skin." growled the beefcake.

"Oh my God! An A.I."

The beefcake curled his lip.

Dan found himself in a security holding room. He was forced to sit behind a table and was as confused as hell. "When it comes to interactive narratives and online reality gaming scenarios, this is where it stops. It's a little too close." Dan reached across and touched the beefcake guard again. "Sorry, just checking if you were there or not and I hadn't walked off with a pair of VR glasses, but no, you really are there." he was handed a cellphone by the beefcake and curled his lip, putting the phone to his ear. "What? What is this? A game? OK, I'll play along. Hi." he masked his nervousness with a sarcastic cockiness.

"This is Ed Williams, Eve's Uncle. Stop your rambling and listen up."

Ed was on one screen and Simmons was on another.

Jaynus viewed them both from the comfort of his chair in the Control Room.

Edogawa stood behind and watched on.

"How ya doin' ma man?" said Jaynus to Ed.

"Hey, I'm Livin' La Vida Loca, but if it ain't me, then it's you, right?" answered Ed. He referred to the many times both him and Jaynus had separately been in near-death scrapes with Brady over the years.

"You got that right, brother. I shoulda known going anywhere in the world with Brady results in heads being broken." Jaynus jested.

"Many a true word." replied Ed.

Dan Simmons was confused. "Um, hello? I'm missing some information."

Brady pressed his cell harder to his ear as he shoved a desk across the floor and against the door. "Yeah? D'you get hold of Simmons?"

"He's on speaker, Brady." said Jaynus

Dan Simmons nervously entered the conversation. "Joe? Firstly, I'd like to-"

"Ain't time for bullshit like that now, Dan. I need a plan or anything to get me outta here. If you can't, tell Eve I love her." Brady felt his time on this earth was soon come to an end. After all he had been through. He didn't want to die. Not like that. Not at the hands of sword wielding maniacs, ready to cut him up. He had been in near-death situations before and was damn sure that dying in a tiny office wasn't going to be the end of him.

"Whoa! Joe. Come on. Don't say that. You can tell her yourself." Dan instantly knew something was up.

"Damn fucking right I will, bone head, but not before I rip your spine outta your goddamn neck." Brady had fight in him yet.

"How vivid. And this is how you ask for my help? Sure. OK. I should know that already." Dan exhaled as his laptop was placed in front of him, having been removed from his rucksack by the beefcake guard.

"Dan, goddamnit! I got fifteen Beni Hanas on my ass, all wanting to turn me into Kobe beef." Brady blurted.

Simmons tapped his laptop keys and did his hacking shit. "For a global power-brand, their software is really lame. Jesus. OK, I got you."

"What d'you mean you got me?"

"I mean I have your location! Jesus." Dan cried.

Brady's print office door was getting seriously splintered up. Images of wild Yakuza were seen peering in.

Through the narrow split door, eyes darted around the sockets like pinballs, searching for Brady.

"Hurry! You found a Teleport machine or anything like that?" yelled Brady.

"What? No. I have located a very cool 3D printer." Dan informed.

BLAM! A shot split a glass touchscreen 'poster' wall.

"Listen, fuckhead, now's not the time to make a goddamn toy!" Brady cried out.

"Would you *please* be quiet? Has the printed got anything inside it?"

"What, like paper?" Brady curled his lip as he glanced across at the printer.

"No! Not paper! A 3D printer doesn't have paper, Brady." replied Dan.

"Well how the fuck would I know?"

"Alright! I'm sorry I asked! I forgot you only know about caveman shit!" Dan blurted. "Look for a lump of plastic. Can you see anything like that?"

Brady dodged an arm that reached out for him as he inspected the 3D printer. "There's a plastic brick inside it. Shall I get it out?"

"No! Leave it. I'm sending a blueprint of a.. Just wait a second." Dan said.

BLAM!

Brady ducked as a crazed yakuza stared at him, with a gun in his hand.

"There's Joeny!" the yakuza cackled.

The 3D printer started to create. Its laser rotated and swirled as it cut a plastic block.

Brady curled his lip and stared at it.

"Joe, is it printing?"

"It's doing something. What's it making? A coffin? Cos that's what I'm gonna need." Brady joked, nervously.

The printer laser spun and zapped separate pieces of plastic. It soon formed the shape of what appeared to be a gun.

"I sent the plans of a Beretta, Joe. It's making you a gun." said Dan, proudly, hoping for Brady's acceptance once more.

"You're kiddin' me?"

"All you gotta do is assemble it." instructed Dan, excitedly.

"Like Legos?" asked Brady.

"Yes, like Legos!" cheered Dan.

The crazed Yakuza split the door and pushed himself into the print room. He held his gun out.

BANG!

Brady ducked and started to jab the yakuza in the face. He then broke his arm and knocked him out.

The yakuza slumped over the splintered door.

"The printer's stopped, dammit!" Brady yelled.

"Then it should be done."

"How do I get the parts, dammit?" Brady, aware of the danger at the broken door, stared at the printer.

"It probably has as lid. A see-through lid! Lift it up and roll it back like a barbeque!" ordered Dan.

Brady slid his fingers under the plastic, protective shield and lifted the lid.

It did indeed roll back on itself like a barbeque lid.

Brady grabbed the plastic parts and quickly assembled them, slotting the colored blocks together to form his favored handgun. A Beretta pistol.

The gun even had plastic bullets.

Brady chuckled and gripped the gun tight. "How the hell does it fire?!"

"It needs a pin. A metal pin! Find one, Brady!" Dan ordered.

Brady looked around the office. He knew a pin wasn't going to just flash before his eyes. Not in that small room where even a goldfish could remember being inside.

The place was clean of metal. It was tidy. That just made Brady even more flustered.

"In all the damn offices in the world, I gotta be in one where there's no fucking pin!"

The slumped yakuza was pulled from the door to reveal more wild faces.

Brady caught his reflection in the broken glass on the wall. He noticed his arm. Brady removed his shirt to reveal his white, wife-beater vest. He quickly retrieved a piece of broken glass from the floor and started to cut his elbow. Brady gritted his teeth. The pain was unbearable, but he knew it was this or die or least die trying. Conscious of the mad-eyed Yakuza eager to reach him, he continued to cut into his skin.

Blood seeped out.

Brady winced as he pinched at the metal pin in his arm and pulled it out., In one swift motion, he hurriedly inserted the metal pin into the plastic gun, just as the yakuza burst inside. Brady shot each and every one of them.

In their necks, chests, arms, heads and guts.

Plastic bullets pierced skin and organs. They cracked bones and skulls with a hard sounding thud as they impacted their target.

Yakuza bodies spun into one another like drunks dancing at a disco. Their blood jetted across the walls and faces as they continued into the office.

Brady was exhausted. He slumped down in a corner and looked at the bodies that were stacked up before him. He chuckled with disbelief.

"Joe? Brady?" said Dan Simmons over the Oshiro phone. "Brady, you alive?"

"I can hear that cowboy laughing, so I'm guessing he's all right." chuckled Ed Williams.

"Ed Williams? Ha, gang's all here." Brady winced. Pained by his elbow, pleasantly surprised by his new gun. He admired it, weighing it in his hand.

"Here for you, man. As I know you would be for me. You OK?" Williams asked Brady.

"I'll be.. Better.. When Joe comes marching home." Brady winced with absolute discomfort. He checked, once more, the bodies of twisted, shot, bloody yakuza piled up and awkwardly went through their stuff. He found a few weapons. He slung an MP5 over one shoulder and a pocketed a Glock. Brady unearthed a pack of Hope cigarettes. It was unclear whether he was more thankful for these than the automatic weapons he had. He clambered over the fallen bodies and back into the open plan office. Brady leaned against the corpses and lit a cigarette.

Suddenly, a spray ejected from somewhere above him and extinguished his cigarette, damping Brady in the process.

Brady sighed and eyeballed his limp cigarette and the soaked packet. He tossed the pack and noticed something sparkle near by.

It was a katana samurai sword.

13. [thirteen]
Slash and Burn

Upon a rooftop, not too dissimilar to the Ark Hills complex, a cool attack helicopter awaited Frederick and Philip.

The pair approached the helicopter, silhouetted against the indigo night sky.

Daniel Simmons watched his screen that depicted the video of Brady apparently killing Kimura. "Whoa! That's disgusting!"

"I know, right. That's why he's up on a murder charge." Jaynus blurted from the Oshiro Control Room.

"No, it's a disgusting sloppy job. The only murder taking place here is on a cheap software effects package. Jesus." stated Simmons, in his geek element.

"In case you haven't noticed, time is a factor, with a capital fucking F. Tell me what's occurring inside that already fucked up skull of

yours, but in a way I can fully understand."
barked Jaynus.

"Someone shot dead the Japanese dude and digitally inserted Brady's face to make it look like he did it. Oh man, so many blatantly obvious mistakes." Simmons explained, in the only way he knew how.

"So explain one of them, idiot." ordered Jaynus.

"Brady is also left handed and is smaller than.."

Jaynus frowned. "Huh? How do they do that? No, don't tell me. OK, so how'd we find out which motherfucker did do it?"

"I'm already on it. I've extracted the original Metadata from the CCTV. I found that it was pulled from the sex clinic. So, it's crudely done, but you'll see the original image in 3, 2.. Now."

A bemused Jaynus, with Edogawa edging closer, looked at a screen that showed the shooting in the fashion health club.

It revealed Philip instead of Brady.

The computer screen flickered.

"Who?"

Ben Brady was at his desk.

Philip's image was on his screen as his computer raced through a facial recognition process.

Ben Brady took a call. "So you knock my sister up and take off? That's how you deal with responsibility? You mother."

IMAGE MATCH: Partial information was seen of Philip on his screen.

Ben's expression revealed panic and worry. It wasn't long before he was running down a corridor with a file in his hand. He reached an elevator and tapped a button.

The door swished open and Ben Brady hurried inside.

Ben ascended a stairwell in lengthy strides and barged through a door at the top. He fixed on his US-Korean colleague who was about to enter another elevator. "Wait! Stop!" Ben prevented the doors from closing, startling the agent.

"You're either unfit or you've seen a ghost." said his colleague.

"Desk job's not really helping so much, but the ghost thing? Kinda hit the nail on the head." Ben Brady quipped, sounding just like his father.

"Yeah. Not following you, Ben."

"The Black Site in Japan? The European prisoner who escaped? You gotta name for him yet?" asked Ben Brady.

The US-Korean agent looked at Ben's highly concerned expression.

The holographic Oshiro logo rotated in the night. Ground level was chaotic.

TV reporters gathered.

 Police struggled to control the area.

It was chaotic. There were abandoned sports cars, luxury vehicles and discarded motorcycles.

Concerned commendation guests left. Many were angered

Members of SWAT discussed tactics near the entrance.

A taxi pulled up outside News Corp, at 1211 Avenue of the Americas in New York City.

Cringe-worthy reporter Bob O'Mally exited the cab and raced inside the building. He was like a rock star. He passed suited suck-ups and attractive production stuff.

Stephanie De Souza, O'Mally's PA, briefed him as he walked. "We have actual footage of him murdering in cold blood and get this, video of him with a hooker."

"Stephanie De Souza, I feel like having sex with you right now." O'Mally insincerely blurted.

"Only your wife's in town and it's not Tuesday." she corrected.

"Forever on the ball. Who's got what?" O'Mally asked.

"Jeb's in the gallery and Richardson has got you a guest."

O'Mally was intrigued. He gave Stephanie a smoldering look.

Jaynus stared at the screens that depicted surveillance images of the then fifty-year old Frederick and a five-year old Philip.

Doors opened and Sarah entered with James and Yoshi Kita, each casting their eyes on the dead Masato and Ringo, not to mention Jaynus' bruised and beaten face.

"I don't know what to ask questions on first." said Sarah.

"I'll help you with your first one. Yes, I am OK. Jaynus replied.

Yoshi bowed his head on seeing Masato.

James eyed the screens.

"Your American guest is innocent." Edogawa stated.

"I've seen the video, Inspector." answered Yoshi.

"TV fakery." stated Edogawa.

Sarah was saddened to see Ringo. She approached his body and closed her eyes briefly. She turned to Jaynus. "Who would frame Joe for murder?"

"I'm guessing one or both of these chisel jawed motherfuckers, but the system kinda froze up before we found out who they are." said Jaynus.

James Kita looked at his digital tablet. "An out-pouring of water has caused a massive short circuit."

"What about the back-up?" asked Sarah.

"I'm no electrician, Sarah."

"But I am." Jaynus straightened.

"With all due respect, Mr. Carter." Yoshi sighed.

"Water conducts electricity. I'm sure you know that, right?" Jaynus was already pissed off with Yoshi.

"Of course, but, listen."

"No, you listen. Think of water as a wire. If water drops on any two parts of a connecting circuit you've short-circuited that circuit, but it's not just water, it's what's in the water. Ions and salts and that kinda shit. Now when something suffers a short-circuit, it causes excessive amounts of current in that particular area. This creates a host of reactions, be it a fire or even an explosion. It's the reactions which makes electronics break. Water can't permanently damage a circuit unless you're operating under high-voltage, which I doubt you are. If your company had used deionized water, there wouldn't be a problem, so don't belittle me or think I'm just a black man who didn't go to Harvard. I know this shit more than you. I'm a fucking electrician." Jaynus said proudly.

Sarah raised her eyebrows to Yoshi.

BOOM! The room suddenly shook. It was due to an explosion from another floor.

They steadied themselves.

Outside the Grand Plaza, Detective Rampo wiped his cut lip. He looked up when he heard the sound of a helicopter. He turned to a senior officer. "We have 14 helicopters and I know that isn't one of them."

Spotlights flared up.

Bullets from mini-guns on an attack chopper, like a Eurocopter Panther, riddled members of a SWAT team.
Missiles took out the SWAT team's chopper on the rooftop of the Oshiro Grand Plaza.

Inside the attack helicopter, Frederick flipped a visor and looked at Philip, the main pilot. "Just the warriors who stand in our way. No innocents. Do you understand?"

Philip looked crazed. He lowered the helicopter upon the roof.

Brady stood alone inside an elevator. Stubble was appearing and he rubbed his cheeks, thinking as he held his newly acquired samurai sword. He caught his reflection and shook his head.

The elevator became transparent.

Brady widened his eyes.

All around him was white and mountainous as the elevator stopped.

Brady cautiously stepped out of the elevator and into a traditional Japanese Onsen hot spring.

There was snow and trees. There was a pool and a fence, with rocky steps that led to a shack.

The digital sky depicted the day as Brady worked his way along the path, towards the wooden shack.

Steam rose from the pool.

Frederick walked from the helicopter, through the holographic Oshiro logo and to a door that Philip held open for him.

Brady entered the onsen shack. His nine-millimeter wast tight in his grip.

A guard lay dead.

Brady located a located a fridge and puts the gun on the side. He grabbed an Oshiro mineral water. As he gulped the water, he went through cupboards.

"Towels, robes, slippers, woman!" Brady suddenly jolted.

A female spa worker leapt out onto him, WOMAN! She crawled her way onto his back and hit him repeatedly. "You're the killer! You're killer!" she screamed.

Brady shook her off and tried his hardest to shut her up.

Brady shakes her off. Tries to shut her up. "No! I'm not. Shut the hell up."

"Killer!" she yelled again. She backed away and pointed at him. The spa worker was frightened by Brady's presence.

A yakuza stepped out from behind a tree. He zipped his fly and listened. He heard the scream of the spa worker.

"Get away from me!"

Brady was anxious. He slapped her and spun her round into a wooden panel, knocking her out cold.

The wooden panel revealed a videophone. It scanned Brady's retina and a CGI Robot Concierge appeared.

"Joe Brady. How may I help you?"

"Uh, Jaynus Carter, please."

Sarah and Jaynus walked through a service corridor. They passed the occasional view of a distant Tokyo and the Bay via glass panels.

"Does he ever talk about me?" asked Sarah.

"That's one to ask your kids." Jaynus replied.

"And when I do, they reel off their forever teenage reply; 'Mom, can we talk about somethin' else?'"

"That's what I was gonna say, except the mom part. In the 20 years I've known him, the only thing he's not straightforward on is his own damn life." Jaynus quipped.

They reached a door.

Sarah's retina was scanned and the door slid open. "I don't quite follow you."

Jaynus followed Sarah inside the server room and saw the servers and electronics and various cables. He jolted when an Oshiro phone sounded out. He took the call as he eyeballed some wires.

"Yo, Jaynus." Brady called out.

"Brady. We were just talking about you." answered Jaynus.

"Who's we?" asked Brady.

"Me and Sarah."

"Sarah? She OK?"

"Yeah. She took me to the main server room. A few electronic issues."

"Got yourself a job?" Brady chuckled.

"Yeah, freelance, but like the commute and just like you, it's a total asshole. Listen up. We got pictures of the real guy who shot Kimura. As well as another dude."

"Who are they? More tattooed pissed off Japanese kids?" Brady sneered.

"No. It's a white boy, with a cheesy grin and Clint Eastwood on a power shake."

"What? You got names?" inquired Brady.

"No. Hence the trip to the server room. Your dip in the pool fucked some shit up, so I gotta rework this and that. Your kid, Ben, sent a file, but it didn't fully come through. Where you held up at?" Jaynus asked.

"Stuck in an Ice Age sequel waiting for Punxatawney Phil." Brady mocked.

"Where is he?" asked Sarah.

"He hung up. He's some place cold."

"Must be the Onsen." Sarah replied.

"He ain't got time to listen to opera. Idiot's gotta think fast. Look alive." Jaynus insisted.

"Not opera. Onsen. It's a traditional Japanese hot spring. The water features are connected. Joe's not too far from here."

Brady wasn't too far at all, however, he was also taking a beating from the yakuza. Brady twisted a towel and wrapped it round the yak's neck. He tried his hardest to choke him. No chance Brady received a punch to the face, but managed to crawl outside the shack. Brady crawls outside. He kicked the yak in the face and rolled down the wooden steps. Brady scrambled to his feet, but the Yak was too fast and quickly upon him.

The yakuza roundhouse kicked Brady into a fence, breaking it.

Brady landed on the snow. He was in tremendous pain. He grabbed a length of splintered wood and slammed it into the yakuza.

The yak fell and shuffled on the snow. He got to his feet and formed a martial arts pose, readying himself, cockily, for Brady.

Brady wiped blood from his nose. "Hey, Bo Jangles. You gonna quit making snow angels and fight like a real boy?" Brady suddenly barged the yak onto the rocks.

The pair struggled.

The yakuza grabbed Brady's wounded elbow, causing him to yell out in absolute agony.

Brady clasped at a piece of splintered wood and rammed it into the Yakuza's arm and twisted it.

It was messy. Blood spattered on the snow and rocks.

Brady held the yakuza's head under the water.

The yakuza's body jerked and his feet shook.

Brady had drowned him. He backed away, exhausted.

Sarah and Jaynus climbed a tunneled ladder. "When you get to the top, it's just a latch and a door." Sarah said.

Brady washed blood from his elbow and tilted his head to a tree that suddenly opened like a door.

Jaynus and Sarah exited the tree.

She stared at the mess of Brady with a loving concern. She was used to seeing him in such a state. Whether that was work-related or alcohol related. Being hurled through a window was all the same to her.

A window was a window.

Brady had look of disappointment. He was forever reluctant, but he was in the zone he knew best.

Jaynus looked at him. "Whoa! What d'you do? Eat him?"

"Who d'you think I am? A member of the Uruguayan rugby team?"

"Are you OK, Joe?"

"Uh, not really, Sarah."

"Ben's online with news we apparently won't like."

"He's knocked somebody up, too? Who is it? Hello Kitty?" mocked Brady.

Wooden panels scrolled down to reveal a large touch screen in the onsen shack.

Jaynus downed some mineral water.

Brady watched Sarah bring up his son on the screen

He looked terrified, both for himself and for his family.

"Mom. Dad. Jaynus. This concerns all of you. All of us."

"What is it, son? You OK?" asked Brady.

"Ben. Honey. What's happened?"

"The file I sent to Jaynus froze up. I.. I'll re-send it.. Dad. His name is Philip Mueller.

Brady scrunched up his face. Had he heard correctly?

An image appeared of Philip's face along with his details.

Name: Philip Mueller. DOB: July 22 1983. Berlin. Education: Black Forest Academy. Kolleg St. Blasien. Employment: Banker OUTLAWED: Turkish-German association Internationale Humanitaere Hilfsorganisation (IHH) Special Forces trained: Turkish Special Forces Command. Freelance Investment Banker.

A scanned photograph of a blonde woman, in a hospital bed, cradling a newborn was seen.

"Who's the baby?"

"That's Philip with his mother." replied Ben Brady.

"So the kid's got daddy issues huh?" Brady quipped.

"Haven't we all? This is his father." said Ben Brady.

A photograph of the baby cradled by his father, Alexander Mueller.

Brady was in total shock. He found it difficult to swallow and almost gagged when he did eventually do so.

Jaynus stared and tried to take it all in. He would look at Sarah and Brady and then Ben Brady on the screen, turn by turn. He scrunched up his face, entirely baffled.

Sarah covered her mouth. "Good God."

Ben Brady continued. "Philip was born Philip Anton Mueller. When Alexander Mueller died – sorry, when *you* killed Alexander, his son, Philip was raised by this guy."

A surveillance photo of Frederick holding the hand of five-year old Philip was seen.

"Frankenstein?" mocked Brady, using his warped humor to deflect his true feelings.

"Frederick Mueller. Grandfather. In nineteen eighty-nine, Frederick was deemed unsafe by Japanese Intelligence. A snatch squad took Frederick off the streets and

imprisoned him for the next thirty years."
informed Ben Brady.

"And he's now dead, right?" asked
Brady.

"No, dad. He's very much alive. Facial
recognition has.. Has.. Identified and placed
both Frederick and Philip Mueller."

"Placed them where, Ben?" quizzed
Brady.

"They're inside the building, dad.
They're inside Oshiro."

Brady did a slow burn to Sarah.

Jaynus shook his head. He remembered
the time when he first encountered Brady
twenty-years before.

The terrorist incident involved
Alexander's younger brother, who targeted
Brady during a heist.

Brady had killed him, just like he had
killed brother several years earlier.

"No. No. Brady. I am an old man. I've
had my time at Mueller Land. You hear me?"
barked Jaynus.

"Joe. Oh, Joe. I'm so sorry." said Sarah.

Brady held Sarah. He was in pain,
mentally, not just physically. "What you sorry
for, huh?"

"It's this company. I know it."

Brady didn't understand. "Sshh."

"Dad? Keep safe. See you when you get
home. OK?" Ben Brady said.

BOOM! The shack shook and the image
was lost.

"I.. We need to get outta here." said
Jaynus.

"Honey? Got an expressway out?" Brady asked.

"Got your sun screen?" Sarah quipped.

14. [fourteen]

Life's a Beach

Bullets zipped this way and that within a white corridor of the Oshiro Grand Plaza.

Smoke canisters rolled along the floor.

SWAT members and yakuza dropped like trees being felled in a forest.

Through the smoke walked Frederick. He was like Darth Vader. Tall and menacing, clutching a machinegun and he strode with great length and shot whoever was in his way.

Philip crawled through an exploded, burned out wall. He looked at his grandfather in awe and the dead strewn about the place. He was in his element and thought he hadn't had a day like that since his grandfather had been taken from him.

It was exactly. A fun day out.

Bob O'Mally sat at his desk as a radio mic was fitted to him. Even he had forgotten why he detested Brady so much. He believed that Brady was an annoying rash that appeared on his skin every so often – or a dose of the flu he caught in the winter months.

Brady's image, with a heading 'Hero Cop Arrested for Murder in Japan' appeared on screen neat him.

O'Mally grinned, smugly. "We'll be back on air in a second. I'll do a brief re-cap and then introduce you."

A floor manager spouted out. "And we're going live in five, four.."

O'Mally ushered the assistant away and straightened. He turned to address the camera. "Welcome back to O'Mally Stars and Stripped. I'm Robert O'Mally. Viewers will be shocked to learn of the breaking news that a former New York Police Detective, considered by many to be a hero, has been arrested for murder in Japan. Joe Brady was of course the man who saved over a hundred lives in the late eighties, during the Oshiro hostage crisis. I'm joined now by a man who was with him on that fateful night, Diamond Thorp. Diamond, welcome."

An African American, who went by the name of Diamond Thorp was a young man when he collected Brady and drove him to meet Sarah thirty years ago. Like everyone else, Diamond got old, too. "Thank you."

"You've spent time in the company of Joe Brady. What can you tell me about his general state of mind?" asked O'Mally.

"His state of mind? He's a straightforward kinda guy. He is what he is."

Eve Brady was on a cross-trainer as she watched O'Mally's show in her apartment.

"And while he was commended on the so-called bravery of his actions, you, however, were not."

"Hey, I'm cool with that. Totally. I did the magazine and TV slots. I earned from them, too. Joe and especially his then wife, were very kind to me. I received healthy compensation from the Oshiro Corporation for the ordeal I endured."

"But it was you and you alone whose brave actions managed to have two terrorists detained and subsequently incarcerated. Those men."

"Leo and uh.."

"Kristyan."

"Yeah, yeah. Those cats." Diamond smiled and nodded.

"What would you say to them?"

"Man, I don't know. I haven't thought about them since rehab. I.. I don't know. Are they even around?"

Those men were around, but they weren't for long.

Outside San Quentin State Prison, Leo, a smart suited African American in his late fifties, walked a free man. He approached an awaiting sedan and asked if they were his ride. He grinned a brilliant smile. One cheek was scarred. Leo clambered into the car and saw his driver was Japanese.

The driver wore shades and his arms were heavily tattooed.

"OK, baby. Let's get some Crystal and Kristyan."

"We got plenty of Crystal." mumbled the driver.

Leo drowned and suddenly hands from behind him garroted him.

The arms were also tattooed, depicting the Kin Kaminari Kai marking.

Leo was choked to death.

The driver smiled and started up the car.

Blue and red lights of medical, police and fire crews swirled around outside the Oshiro Grand Plaza.

Helicopters buzzed overhead.

It was still a mixed crowd, but cops and Special Forces took control.

Rampo turned to see his boss and colleague Edogawa being carried out by medics.

He shooed the medics away and adjusted a newly placed sling. "The American is innocent. Rampo-san. Kita are Kin Kaminari Kai."

Rampo frowned, naively.

An explosion of leather and red lighting was ever present in a secret cigar room of the Oshiro Grand Plaza.

Psychedelic holograms were projected onto huge waterfalls and dancing puppets and statues rose out of the water.

Old-timer Yakuza smoked and relaxed with one another.

Frederick entered. He narrowed his eyes and looked at the men before him.

The men were both shocked and in awe of Frederick's size.

"If they're not real cigars, I'll kill you all." said Frederick.

A bodyguard faced off with Frederick, but he was punched in the gut and Frederick grabbed him by the throat.

Frederick squeezed him, lifting him up and choking him. "Now which are you? Kin Kaminari Kai or Kura Sasori Kai?" Frederick dropped the man to the floor. "You know what? I don't care. I just want to know where the Kita secret room is. Your Bodaiji. The one with the all the history. Show your face, Kita." he continued. "Let a Kita show their face." Frederick ordered in Japanese.

Philip trained his gun like a member of SWAT as he stood behind his grandfather. "We can look their pictures up. They'll be on the board website."

"Now what fun would that be?" said Frederick, looking at the Japanese men around him.

Screens flickered and depicted Philip with a 'wanted' in Japanese and English warning. A video loop of Philip killing Kimura was shown.

"No. No this can't be. How?" Philip was shocked to see this. More so than the old-timers around him.

The Robot Concierge made an announcement. "Attention. Joe Brady is innocent. He is a guest of Oshiro. He did not kill Governor Honzo Kimura. This man, Philip

Mueller, is wanted." The message was repeated in Japanese.

The Yakuza exchanged looks.

Bodyguards pulled guns and took aim at Frederick and Philip.

"Opa." said Philip.

"Relax, Philip, my grandchild. Patience. Know Forty-eight year old George Kita stood up. He straightened and faced Frederick. "Stop. I am Kita. George Kita. There is no secret history room. From your accent, I think I know who you are. You're a Mueller. Am I correct?"

Frederick lit a cigar. He pulled on it and exhaled. "I'm Frederick Mueller."

"Are you the eldest, Mueller-san?"

"Hai. I am eighty years old." replied Frederick in Japanese.

"What you're seeking.."

"I'm seeking money and Brady." Philip interrupted.

"Shut your mouth!" Frederick barked in German.

"What you're seeking is not in the building, Mr. Mueller." stated George Kita.

Frederick exhaled his smoke and smirked, knowingly.

"Grandfather, I will not allow you to do this!" Philip cracked George Kita around the face and exited the room.

Frederick turned. He was disappointed.

On another tunneled ladder, Brady, Jaynus and Sarah climbed.

"Let me look first, OK? Stay back." said Brady.

The indoor Oshiro beach was magnificent and extremely surreal.

Bars, huts, wooden paths and white sand and of course, an ocean bay.

The digital sky appeared ever so realistic.

A jet ski skipped across the water, passing volleyball players and sunbathers.

Doors swished open and Philip set foot on the sand. He was packing some major heat.

A volley ball was flung in the air.

Philip blasted the ball.

People screamed and started to flee.

Oshiro guards appeared helpless and wary.

"And what are you guys gonna do?" Philip yelled.

A rock flipped up and Brady clambered out. He looked around and brushed sand from his hands. He saw people running in panic and then noticed Philip, walking across the sand with his guns.

Philip locked eyes with Brady.

Brady aimed a machinegun at him and slowly straightened.

Philip raised his hands and started to walk towards Brady.

"Stay where you are. I said don't move!" Brady shouted.

There was just five feet between them.

Philip stopped and stared.

Brady was wary. He looked Philip up and down.

Philip's eyes glazed over. His face scrunched up and he began to cry. "You killed my father!"

"Back away, Philip." yelled Brady.

Philip sobbed and lowered his head. He dropped a .45 to the sand.

Brady couldn't work it out.

Philip fell to his knees.

"Hey. Hey, kid. C'mon let it go." Brady said.

Philip suddenly looked up. He was as angry as hell. "Let it go? You can go back to whatever rock you crawled out under."

"That one there. Actually." Brady curled his lip, cautious of Philip.

Philip suddenly threw sand into Brady's face and knocked him to the ground. He straddled him and presses an RPG against Brady's neck.

Brady struggled, squinting due to the sand in his eyes.

Jaynus looked up from the rock-tunnel. He fixed on Brady and scrambled out to assist him. He grabbed Philip, but was elbowed in the face, knocking him backwards.

Philip choked Brady.

Brady squinted up at the digital sun, but was suddenly overshadowed.

A silhouette towered above. It was Frederick. He pulled Philip from Brady and threw him to the sand. He looked down on Brady and extended his hand to him.

Brady looked at it and pondered. He reached up.

Frederick helped Brady to his feet.

"Brady?" Jaynus was confused and extremely wary.

Philip was furious. He was enraged. "Opa! This is Joe Brady! He killed my father! Your son! He killed both your sons!"

"And it ends. He's not the cause." Frederick stated.

"He's my cause! My cause! My pain!" Philip screamed.

Sarah peered up from the rock.

Philip noticed her. He suddenly rolled on the sand and grabbed his .45.

Frederick pushed Brady aside.

BLAM! Frederick was shot in his side. He winced with pain and gritted his teeth. Frederick punched Philip in the face and retrieved a shotgun.

Philip screamed! He let rip with his machinegun and shot everything in his sight.

Palm trees and digital screens were torn and shattered.

The huts and beach bar splintered.

SWAT and a handful of Yakuza appeared. Some returned fire. Some dove out the way of gunfire.

Philip was shot in the chest. He roared and wheezed, eyeing up his bulletproof vest. He pulled his RPG, extending it and fired a rocket upwards.

BOOM!

The digital blue sky ceiling cracked and fizzled.

Jaynus looked up and ran as the ceiling split.

The Eurocopter Panther suddenly appeared as it fell through roof.

Brady pulled Frederick to the sea.

SMASH! BOOM!

The helicopter smashed on the shore and exploded into a ball of flame!

Sarah ducked as flames raced across the tunnel entrance.

Philip sprayed bullets and took out SWAT team members with ease. He took a dive and disappeared from sight.

Brady trod in the water with Frederick.

Flames from the chopper and its debris drifted around them

Brady spotted a speedboat.

Philip saw Brady and Frederick near the boat. He fixed on a jet ski and flipped the RPG sight and took aim with another rocket.

Frederick clambered into the speedboat. His side was bleeding.

Brady checked the boat. He saw a parachute attached to the middle of the boat and noticed Frederick glancing round.

"GET DOWN! Brady GET DOWN!"

WHOOSH!

A rocket raced across the water.

Brady ducked as the rocket passed over him and cracked the horizon.

Brady detached the anchor and leapt into boat as bullets pierced the water. Brady turned to see Philip on the jet ski.

Philip pulled the throttle and sprayed his machinegun with the other hand. "Grandfather! Kill Brady!"

Brady started up the speedboat and raced it over the fake sea

Frederick clutched his bloody wound.

Brady glances round. "It's raining helicopters and Muellers again, Joe." He tightened and revved the boat towards the horizon.

The boat is shot up by Philip's bullets, but was distancing itself from Philip.

The throttle suddenly came off in Brady's hand.

"Shit!"

"That not meant to happen?" Frederick asked.

"No!"

Jaynus looked on through the flames as he stood on the beach. "Slow it down, Brady!"

Sarah peered from the rock. She was horrified.

Frederick squinted and shuffled back. He held on tightly. "Brady? Do it."

Brady nodded. He stared dead-ahead. "Just when I thought it safe to go back in a high building."

The sea was ending.

The cracked, fake horizon loomed closer. Closer.

SMASH!

Outside the Oshiro Grand Plaza, the speedboat smashed through the windows of the highest floor.

Brady and Frederick were of course inside as the boat jetted across like a plane! Glass glistened. It glided along and then the wind took held of the parachute and started to float down!

Wind blew through the broken windows, leaving Philip in total disbelief. He looked back to the shore and saw flames and also Jaynus and Sarah. He narrowed his eyes.

Jaynus pulled Sarah from the tunnel. "I.. I don't know if he's dead or alive, but I gotta.."

"Jaynus. Jaynus. There's a floor. A room. New technologies. Just tell the elevator this code: 9136." Interrupted Sarah.

"9136. He'll be OK. It will be OK." Jaynus said positively.

Sarah wiped a tear from her cheek.

Jaynus smiled, but jolted back to see Philip approach them.

Philip stepped over the flames. His arm was set on fire and he casually patted it out and grabbed Sarah, aiming his gun at Jaynus. "I know your face, too."

Jaynus held out his hands. "Hey, I didn't kill your father."

"What about my uncle?" Philip stated.

"No. No he tried to kill me. I was innocently brought into his sick, twisted game."

"Well, I had nobody to play games with therefore I don't play them."

Sarah struggled.

BANG!

Philip shot Jaynus in the shoulder, sending him backwards and rolling out of sight.

"No!" Sarah cried out.

Philip twisted Sarah round and pressed the barrel up into her chin. "Yes."

"Do you make your mother proud?"

"I don't know. I don't have one. Will you be my mommy?" Philip cackled an odd laugh and then snarled.

Sarah was extremely fearful.

Amongst the island grounds of the Oshiro Grand Plaza, the parachuting speedboat slowly drifted down to the undergrowth, breaking branches and landed with a thud.

Brady bumped his head.

Frederick ejected a cartridge from the pump-action. He sliced it open and lifted his shirt, emptying the gunpowder onto his wound. He then struck a match and brought the flame to the powder.

FIZZ!

Frederick sealed his wound, gritting his teeth with pain.

Brady stared at him.

"I knew our paths would cross one day, Brady. I sensed it."

"Yeah, kinda like deja vu. Right now I'd really like to sense a bottle of fuckin' Aspirin." Brady was tired. Mentally and physically drained.

Frederick pumped back the shotgun.

Brady swallowed. Shit.

"Relax. I'm not interested in killing you. I'm here for something else." Frederick said, as he clambered out of the boat and through the long grass.

Brady curled his lip and squinted at Frederick's silhouette. "Muellers. Never just about one thing." Brady painfully stepped out of the boat and looked around.

Darkness and long grass and a distant Oshiro building, both glistening and smoking in the distance.

Brady followed Frederick through the long grass.

15. [fifteen]
The Bodaiji

It was still daytime in New York City.

Bob O'Mally swiveled on his chair to a satellite video-link of a man enjoying retirement in a nice garden.

Loren Carr was a former Police Captain who had experienced a great deal of stress due to Brady and an incident that occurred in the early nineties. He took early retirement because of it.

O'Mally was dragging every one he damn well could from Brady's past. Anybody who had grief with him, O'Mally wanted to put them on TV. Anything to make Brady look guilty.

"Look, I agree with you on that point. Don't get me wrong. First impressions. But let me tell you this. Joe Brady did what others wouldn't do. He showed out and out bravery when I met him. Sure he was a complete asshole, with a total disregard for anything politically correct, however, when it came to putting others first, he was right up there with the best of 'em. His wife's life was at risk, like hundreds of others were on those planes. The love he had for her. Passion and gut instinct drives that man. Passion and gut instinct." reeled off the former Captain.

"You say that, Captain, but we've obtained video footage that will surely say otherwise." replied O'Mally.

Bright lights flickered.

Brady entered a Tokyo subway carriage, which rumbled and began to shake.

It was empty except for a hot female passenger.

She sat opposite and crossed her legs, in a short skirt.

He looked at her.

She suddenly started to attack him.

A dome camera filmed him. He pushed the woman away.

She started to grope him, practically clawing at his clothes.

Brady grabbed her wrists.

She tried to resist him and twisted her body, but he was too strong for her.

Brady ripped open her shirt, revealing her huge breasts in a fancy black bra. He pulled at her skirt, which dropped and showed her matching panties.

The car rumbled. Through strobes that would give people seizures in the cinema, Brady's neck was kissed.

Uncharacteristically, he felt her up.

The subway car stopped.

The lights appeared in full and the doors opened.

The woman straightened. She collected her clothes, bowed to Brady and exited the carriage. She passed a sign that read 'SEX-CLUB SUBWAY'.

Eve Brady shook her head with disbelief, having just seen her father depicted on O'Mally's television show in a bizarre sexual manner for not just the entire country to see, it was even being broadcast live on the internet. Eve muted the TV and dialed a number on her phone. "It's me. I don't wanna fight. If you wanna come back home and be part of a proper family then you have to do something first."

Daniel Simmons was of course on the other end of the line. "I don't think being part of your family will ever be considered proper, but sure, baby, go ahead."

Smoke bellowed out of the roof and drifted across the Tokyo skyline.

Fire was present on various floors. Flames flickered wildly due to cracked windows, pierced pipes and punctured air conditioning.

Handfuls of yakuza were led into police vans outside. Some gestured to the roof and then rounded the building.

Mei Kita was there. She was shoved by George Kita, who looked at his brother, Yoshi. "I'm not getting in the car!"

"Get her in the car." George barked.

"No! We'll be stopped on the bridge and arrested for committing fraud. We've concealed our identities. We're a yakuza front!" Mei blurted.

George went to slap her, but Yoshi gripped his wrist.

Mei took her chance and suddenly made a dash for it.

"In the car. All of you. In!" George yelled.

Edogawa had his cuts tended to as he sat on the back of an ambulance.

Rampo leaned in. It was a baptism of fire regarding his policing experience.

Edogawa noticed all of the Kita family being led to awaiting limousines. He sat up.

Rampo straightened, taking note of his mentor's eye-line.

"Kita. Kita. Kita." Edogawa grunted, with disgust.

Jaynus traveled in an elevator within the Oshiro smart building. He gripped his katana sword tightly.

The Robot Concierge detected that he needed urgent medical assistance.

"No fucking shit. I've been shot! Take me to technology 9136." Jaynus yelled, angrily. He looked in an absolute mess.

Amongst the long grass, Frederick walked in the moonlight like a figure from Greek mythology or a statue that had been brought to life.

Brady wasn't too far behind him. He was confused, yet curious as to where he was headed to.

The occasional fire burned on patches of long grass.

Frederick turned. "The Bodaiji." he continued, walking out of sight.

"Bo-da what?" asked Brady. He pushed through the long grass and stopped. Ahead of him was a pathway.

A Bodaiji was a family temple made of stone and wood where generation after generation took care of their dead. There was even a shrine inside. It's name simply meant Buddhist enlightenment.

"A bodi temple. A place where you look after your dead. Look after your history. This is the Kita clan's bodaiji." explained Frederick.

Brady watched Frederick kick open the gate. The clang of metal echoed into the night.

Frederick walked along a path. He located an entrance by some wooden Oshiro labeled crates.

Jaynus entered the 9136 Technology room within the Grand Plaza. He was in awe of the various technologies around him. He saw a single-man electric helicopter, like the Hirobo.

"Jaynus Carter. Welcome to nine one three six. Would you like a tour?" asked the Robot Concierge.

"No. I wanna ride that cool helicopter motherfucker and find Joe Brady!" Jaynus bellowed.

Frederick entered the Kita-Clan Bodaiji Temple.

Moonlight shone through the door, creating shards of white light through the wooden cracks. The light picked up dust, which twinkled in the air as it floated around the temple.

Inside was colorful. Golden. Magnificent.

Katana swords, fixed on the walls, glistened, capturing the light of the moon and other reflecting objects inside.

Sculptures, pottery, framed, old sepia and black and white photographs lined the walls, between woodblock prints and statues.

The place was like a museum.

Frederick viewed the photographs in turn. He studied them and felt like his life's work was coming to a fruitful end.

Brady entered and watched Frederick study the pictures. Brady thought he had accidently followed a great explorer who had just busted open a Pharaoh's tomb, deep within an Egyptian pyramid.

"My Great Grandfather, Jacob Mueller. He served in the Prussian army." Frederick gestured to a photograph on one wall.

"I.. I don't understand." Brady was confused.

Frederick admired the art and approached another photograph. "In eighteen-sixty-one, Jacob arrived in Japan. Look. This is my Great Grandfather." he gestured again for Brady to look with him. "He spoke Malay.

Brady stepped next to Frederick and looked at the photograph.

The photograph was in a near-perfect condition. It depictured a tall European man. He was Jacob Mueller and was stood with a group of old school Samurai.

The Samurai looked proud to be photographed.

"Why was your Great Grandfather in Japan?" Brady asked, curiously, frowning as he tried to take in the overwhelming nature of the situation. He had no idea German people flocked to Japan to work during the eighteen hundreds. Many were sought after for their knowledge in the fields of medicine. Others were like Frederick's Great Grandfather.

"He was an arms dealer. He counseled a Daimyo, a territorial warlord of the Kita-clan." Frederick explained.

"Waitaminute. You're telling me your family's known the Kita family for over what.. A hundred and fifty years?" Brady was baffled.

"One hundred and fifty seven." corrected Frederick.

"Jesus Christ." Brady exclaimed.

"Actually, it's more like Buddha." chuckled Frederick. "It is said that Kita and Mueller share the same bloodline. We are one. If that is the case, so is our wealth. I don't see a likeness, my self, but I'm open to persuasion. It was to be the modernization of Japan."

Brady couldn't believe what he was hearing, let alone what he saw on the wall. He tried to take it all in, but it was too overwhelming comprehend. He just couldn't make sense of it.

Frederick took an eighteen-sixties French rifle. "Jacob Mueller channeled thousands of French rifles for the Kitas, but he was soon set upon by Samurai, who were against foreigners. His most valuable stock *taken* by the Kitas. They betrayed us. They stole my birthright." Frederick was becoming angry. He rounded a pillar.

Brady stepped round and saw a Gatling gun from eighteen sixty-two.

The gun glistened.

Frederick looked at in absolute awe. "My birthright."

"This is what your feud is all about? A fucking Gun? A Gatling Gun, right?" Brady curled his lip with disbelief.

"Wrong. Not just a gun. The *money*. The Kita clan made their fortune from this. Look at them now! Look! They're a global super brand." Frederick's voice boomed.

"So what do you want? Mueller Land?" Brady said, sarcastically.

Frederick moved the gun upon its wheels slightly. "Prices varied for these. Jacob sold one for nine thousand dollars. He had twelve of them. Today's calculations have that figure at around twenty million dollars. An unimaginable amount for those times, let alone now."

Brady curled his lip. "So the jealously and bitterness of the past is handed down to the next generation, is that it? Each Mueller son sets out to steal what they believe is theirs, huh?" Brady was slowly working it all out.

"It is theirs! Like it is mine!" Frederick bellowed.

"Well, good luck getting that past customs." Brady mocked. Brady turned to see Frederick pushing the Gatling gun into the main temple area.

"If you had not interfered thirty years ago, we wouldn't be here!" Frederick stated.

"I think about that all the time!" Brady was pissed.

"So what are you going to do?" Frederick shouted.

Brady looked at the gun and then turned around. He swallowed and rolled his tongue around inside his mouth, filling out his cheeks and gums and he thought hard.

The sound of a gathering was heard outside the temple.

"Leave the party?" Brady said quietly.

Frederick looked past Brady and saw dozens of yakuza. "Get back!" Frederick cranked the Gatling gun.

The noise was unimaginably loud, disturbingly in fact.

Brady gritted his teeth as he took an instant dislike to the sound immediately. He felt like vomiting and shielded himself as bullets were let loose.

Yakuza with swords and guns were riddled with bullets as Frederick pushed the Gatling gun out of the temple.

The temple was being shot at.

Debris rained down.

Yakuza bodies were torn apart. Some shook like marionettes with their strings cut, as they were shot.

Bones were shattered.

Arms and legs were ripped off.

Torsos split open.

Heads exploded and cracked.

It was complete carnage as blood soaked into the earth and the cries and screams of the dying echoed in the darkness.

Brady crawled out. Bullet shells pinged around him as he took cover behind wooden crates.

One crate was suddenly splintered by gunfire. Shards of wood scattered in all directions.

Brady winced as he received a wooden splinter in his hand. As he pulled the bloody piece from out of his skin he glanced at something that was once housed within the crate.

Amongst the long grass, more yakuza appeared. They were angry and wielded swords.

The war was in full swing.

Warriors of all social classes had come together to fight. Many had come to hunt Brady down. Some had been ordered by the Kitas to track Frederick and rid him from the earth. Others simply had a wild thirst to kill.

Brady briefly reminisced to the night of hell in nineteen seventy-seven and the New York City blackout.

The burning fires in the long grass like smoldering trashcans.

The buildings that were on fire.

The oncoming groups of people, wild and frenzied.

He winced and clutched his chest, pained. He took a deep breath and gripped the weapon tighter.

Jaynus strapped himself into the one-man helicopter device.

It was more like a jetpack than the look of a helicopter.

Lights flared up and the wall of the Grand Plaza opened out.

A platform slid Jaynus out and round.

Gunfire could be heard from the rough ground below.

"Tracking Joe Brady. Joe Brady located. Jaynus Carter, do you still wish to join Joe Brady?"

"Yes. Yes!" Jaynus screamed.

"Auto-pilot initiated."

The helicopter started up and took off into the night.

"No! No!" Jaynus panicked.

Philip exited a service door amongst some construction and noticed he was on the edge of the island grounds. He squinted to see to the long grass a short distance away.

Frederick winced as his body was punctured by several bullets. His clothing tore apart and the fabric became soaked with his blood immediately. He gritted his teeth and continued to crank the Gatling gun as more yakuza advanced towards him.

Brady pulled something from within the long wooden crate.

It was a chainsaw Katana!

Brady brought the device to life with a roar and strode forth. He tore into the oncoming enemy.

Blood and limbs flew and Brady pushed through the long grass.

Some yakuza fled the area, yelling at others to do the same.

Blood escaped Frederick's mouth. He dropped to his knees.

The firing stopped. Just the whirring of an empty Gatling gun was heard.

"BRADY!"

Brady was bloody, too and turned around.

Frederick slumped over the Gatling gun and loosened his grip. He wanted to keep hold of it. It didn't matter to him that he was severely injured. He just wanted his hand to touch it.

Brady stepped to him. He pitied Frederick, but oddly respected him. Brady gripped Frederick's hand and placed his other hand on the gun.

Frederick smiled. "My way." Frederick became limp. Like a fallen warrior, he was dead.

Brady looked at him for several seconds in silence.

A gentle breeze moved the long grass.

Frederick was at peace.

For a moment, Brady thought it was all over.

"Opa!" Philip cried out.

Brady bolted round to see Philip.

Tears were in his eyes. He was sad for the loss of his Grandfather.

A yakuza appeared and turned.

Philip stared.

"Here's your inheritance, kid." Brady sighed.

Philip shot the yakuza dead and raised his gun at Brady. He pulled the trigger.

Click. Empty.

Five yakuza stepped out from the long grass.

Philip held his stare on Brady and then quickly headed into the darkness. He lowered himself into the long grass and tried to make sense of his situation. He was completely distraught. His entire plan, breaking his grandfather out of the secret prison, pitting yakuza faction against yakuza faction and working a way to gain Kita's Oshiro wealth was in utter ruin. Then of there was Joe Brady. He felt his entire life had been cursed because of him.

Brady had killed his father, Alexander. He had killed his uncle several years later and now Philip believed Brady was responsible for the death of his grandfather, Frederick.

Philip was a lost soul. He felt his grandfather had been the one to instill his core values.

Frederick had introduced Philip to the various cultures of life.

Philip barely got to know his father, Alexander, before he was taken from him. Brutally killed by Brady thirty years before.

Philip became more and more angry. He saw a glistening blade on the ground and retrieved it.

A shadow loomed over him and Philip looked up. His eyed locked with a yakuza and in an instant Philip leapt up with his newly acquired knife and slit the throat of the yakuza. He slashed the man's neck hard and with tremendous force, that the head was practically severed. Philip strode through the grass, wild-eyed and disappeared into the night.

In the mini helicopter, Jaynus headed down to the long grass beside Brady. "Brady!"

Brady looked up. Just when he couldn't be more freaked out, he saw Jaynus floating down in the electric contraption with a sword in his hand.

The yakuza looked just as surprised.

"What the ff.." Brady mumbled.

The mini helicopter landed and Jaynus retrieved a mega head-rush

He wiped his bloody nose as he unstrapped himself and stumbled out, swiping his sword about the place. He took out four yakuza in no time at all.

The lone yakuza looked at Jaynus, then at Brady. He dropped his sword and ran.

Jaynus glanced at the helicopter and chuckled with disbelief. He looked at Brady and the chainsaw katana his grasp.

"You've got a chainsaw katana." Jaynus stated.

Brady was bemused by Jaynus's entrance. He glanced at his chain-sword. "Yeh, it's like.. Training wheels."

Jaynus eyed the destruction and the dead Frederick in the darkness. "Mueller. He's got Sarah."

"Fuck. Where?"

16. [sixteen]
The Oshiro Train

A single width train carriage on a rail was reading itself on the underground service rail of the Oshiro Corporation. It had a transparent roof and resembled a theme-park ride.

Sarah was up front.

Philip was sat behind.

The train began to race through the tunnel just as Brady and Jaynus arrived at the entrance.

Brady saw the train distancing. "Dammit!"

"Hey, Brady?" Jaynus gestured Brady to look up.

Brady saw Mei climb down a ladder nearby.

She stepped on the platform and turned. "Going somewhere?"

Mei turned and looked at the mess of Brady and Jaynus. She exhaled. "I was going to the city."

"Thing is, train's just left." Brady stated.

"We have track maintenance." Mei replied.

Brady and Jaynus frowned.

The Oshiro Maintenance Train confused Brady, whose wounds were being tended to by Mei.

Jaynus tried to clamber inside it. He was also beaten, bloody and hurt. "Where do I sit?"

"You're staying outta this one." Brady said to him.

"What?"

"You heard me."

"Brady, I always hear you. That's the problem. I'm coming with you." Jaynus insisted.

"No. You're not. You've... We've come a long way." Brady sighed, wondering if that was a fairwell statement.

"No shit. fifteen hours on a plane."

"I meant in general. Over the years. I know I've not been easy to be around, but I just wanna say.. thank you. For everything." Brady extended his hand.

Jaynus fixed on it. He rolled his eyes up to meet Brady's and nodded his head. He gripped Brady's hand and pulled him close. "That was more a rehearsal speech for Sarah, you dumb fucking asshole. Go do what you do and leave me to bleed in peace. Shoulda stayed in a Holiday Inn."

Brady sneered and smirked at his friend, Jaynus, who nodded at him.

At the Tokyo end of the platform, Philip yanked Sarah from the train and held his gun to her. He pushed her and pulled a cellphone. "Have any Kita been arrested?"

There was a police blockade on the bridge from Tokyo to Oshiro.

The police officer, Ken, discreetly spoke on his cellphone, walking away from the flashing, swirling lights. "Not yet. They're on the bridge." Ken looked at the Kita limousines that had been forced to stop further on the bridge.

Philip gritted his teeth. He was pissed. He shoved Sarah forth. "Don't let the police arrest them." He beeped out and took hold of Sarah. He eyed his surroundings.

"Why don't you want the Kita's arrested?" Sarah asked.

Philip yanked her head back by her hair. He worked the gun around her face. "Why? Why?! If any of the Kita family is arrested, then all their assets will be frozen. This includes shares in Oshiro Corp. They can be arrested one by one until the cows come home, but not until I have bought their shares, which I presume, with all this negative publicity, they are at their lowest."

"And you think buying them up will get you a place on the board?" Sarah quipped.

"I think me buying them up is none of your God damn business. Now, where is the exit?" Philip pressed the barrel of his gun into her forehead. He released his grip on Sarah and stared at her, disturbingly.

Brady and Mei rode the maintenance train.

It wasn't as flashy as the official Oshiro train, but it worked just as well.

"Where does the train stop?" Brady called out.

"Oshiro own a private bar. The train stops in its basement. It was a quicker route to the city." answered Mei.

"Or to evade capture by police." Brady mumbled. His words lost in the wind as the train headed into the darkness.

Upon the bridge, SWAT and police closed in on the Kita limousine.

Doors opened and members of the Kita family were removed.

Yoshi, James, George and their sister, along with another brother.

Detectives Edogawa and Rampo exited their car, which wasn't too far away.

Ken lowered a pair of binoculars. "Kita removed from limousine."

"Then do what is asked of you." Philip ordered down the other end of the line.

Ken closed his eyes briefly. He re-opened. He beeped out his cell and then keyed in the number 31955.

Beneath the bridge a digital device signaled a green light.

BOOM!

The bridge exploded.

Cars, police officers and other vehicles lifted into the air.

Some were flung into the water below.

Edogawa ducked behind a flaming car with Rampo.

The Kita family spread, saving themselves. They were no longer a priority.

Sarah and Philip stepped to a secure door. The Oshiro glowed red on the wall beside it.

"Open the door." Philip ordered.

"I can't." Sarah replied.

"Open the door." Philip said more forcefully.

"I can't. I don't have access."

"You work for Oshiro." Philip pressed.

"But I'm not a Kita. This system is coded only for members of the Kita family."

"Contact one." Philip barked.

"What, and ask them to text message me a picture of their eye? It's a retina scan." Sarah explained.

Philip eyed the door. He kicked it. He was incredibly angry and turned to think.

The maintenance trained pulled into the platform a little further back.

Brady and Mei clambered out the train and onto the platform. They began walking along, when Brady stopped. He stared, curiously and slowly smiles. He saw Sarah a few meters ahead. "Sarah! You OK, honey?"

Sarah formed a pained smile. She shook her head.

Brady frowned and became alert when Philip stepped out of an archway.

Brady turned.

BANG!

Brady was shot in the side of the head.

"JOE!" Sarah screamed.

Mei widened her eyes with shock as Brady fell to the platform ground.

The side of his head was extremely bloody.

"JOE! Oh, no. Oh my God, no!" Sarah cried.

Philip walked with lengthy strides for Mei.

She turned, but he grabbed her hair and yanked her backwards.

Philip towered above Brady and kicked him down onto the rails below. He dragged Mei to the secure door.

"WHAT HAVE YOU DONE?" Sarah yelled.

Philip slapped Sarah around the face. He then grasped Mei's cheeks and forced her to look at the retina scan on the door.

Mei closed her eyes. "No. No, I won't."

"YES YOU WILL! YOU WILL!" Philip shouted.

"No. It's not just this door."

"Mei. Mei, please. Just do as he says." Sarah insisted.

"Yes, Mei. Do as I say. Open it."

"NO!" Mei screamed back.

"Oh, so you think you'll slow me down by not complying? I don't think so." Philip squeezed her face.

Sarah looked away. She was distressed.

17. [seventeen]
TV Fakery

The TV studio cameras were ready for O'Mally, who breathed fast and heavy.

He was enjoying his moment.

The floor manager stepped up with a Tom Sizemore looking guy.

He was smart, slick and in his fifties.

"Ten seconds from commercial and.."

"Who's this?" asked O'Mally.

"I'm Bill. Bill Clayton."

"Congratulations. And?"

The man was holding back his anger, which he quickly released. "And? And fuck you, asshole! I was one of the hostages on that night in Oshiro Plaza, you low-life piece of shit. Joe Brady saved my fucking life! I owe him! I owe him!"

O'Mally stepped back as beefy security man-handled the man out of shot, leaving O'Mally startled and unready for the cameras.

The screen behind him flickered.

"It was when Joe Brady was a rookie officer in the New York Police Department that he met the woman who was to be his long suffering wife. Sarah Kita. A spate of violent assaults on female students in the Upper West Side area of the city, Kita was used by Brady as bait. He.." O'Mally paused his monologue and turned to his large screen.

The screen depicted a lone human head.

It was a disguised CGI Daniel Simmons.

"We're experiencing some technical difficulties at.." O'Mally was confused and looked around his studio for answers.

"Attention viewers. You are all being deceived." Simmons' voice was disguised, too.

"What's going on here?" O'Mally blurted.

"Dick. O'Mally. Just like framing Joe Brady for murder is extremely capable.." said Simmons, working his magic from the other side of the world.

An image of Brady's face appeared and was exchanged for Philip's on the Kimura murder video on the screen.

O'Mally tapped his microphone. He shrugged.

"..so is placing your host.." Simmons continued.

An image of O'Mally, from his brief report on the shore of the Indian Ocean, appeared for viewers to see.

The sky was removed to reveal a green-screen backdrop. It was all studio work.

"Turn it off! Stop it!" O'Mally panicked. He was frustrated.

Daniel Simmons continued. "You see. Robert O'Mally was never in the Indian Ocean. He wasn't even held hostage by Somali Pirates."

Images of CGI Somali Pirates were shown on screen. They were actors, in a television studio.

"Stop! I need air. Fresh air." O'Mally stood up and removed his radio microphone.

The CGI head of Daniel Simmons laughed.

The production crew were all confused.

A sedan screeched to a halt outside the television studio.

Eve Brady, with her swollen ankles, exited the car and arched her back. "Feet swollen like my aunt's. When will I feel normal again?"

Graying former Detective Lamb, one of Brady's ex colleagues in the department, stuck his head out of the driver's window. "When your kid is in college." he replied to her. He then gestured her to look.

O'Mally pushed the door open and stepped out onto the street. He breathed heavily and was incredibly anxious. He lowered his head and then noticed a shadow in front of him. He looked up to see he was face to face with Eve Brady.

Even punched him hard in the mouth. "That's thirty years of built up courage, you son of a bitch."

"Who.. Who are you?" O'Mally said, clutching his jaw. His mouth was bleeding.

"A very hormonal Eve Brady."

O'Mally sighed and closed his eyes.

"Daddy's girl all right. Ready to go buy chocolate chips now?" Lamb said.

"Yes, I'm ready." Eve clambered back into the sedan.

18. [eighteen]
Holo-Oke

An illuminated Oshiro logo was fixed on the wall.

Philip dragged Sarah along a corridor, BEEP.

A door opened.

Philip and Sarah reached some stairs and ascended them.

Brady was still slumped on the rails. He opened on eye and turned his head to look at the platform. In his blood-soaked clothes, he painfully clambered onto the platform, with a nine millimeter in his grasp. "Man, I could do with some fucking Aspirins." His head bloody, his tired body walked to the secure door.

Mei was lying dead on the platform by the door.

Brady squatted down beside her. "No. Jesus. Mei? Mei, can you hear me? Mei? It's Joe Brady." He rolled her onto her back.

One eye was missing from her socket. She had also been shot in the stomach.

Brady cringed at the sight and glanced up at the door housing the retinal scan. Brady knew there was no other way round it. He held Mei's body up and gently supported her face. With his other hand, he opened her one eye.

The eye was scanned and the door opened.

Philip stepped to a computer terminal.

Sarah stood behind him. A thousand and one thoughts race around her mind.

Philip brought up stocks and shares, then graphs and banking figures. "Yes!" he cried.

"You obviously don't need me." Sarah sighed.

"Hmm?" Philip was too into the computer than to be concerned by Sarah.

Sarah looked to a bar top. She saw Mei's eyeball and the optic nerve. She stepped away, gently picked up the eyeball and quickly scanned it.

Suddenly, the voice of the Robot Concierge sounded out, alerting Philip.

"Mei. Great to have you back! Your rock hit classics are about to play! Remember, just say a keyword and I'll play the song!"

Bad Moon Rising by Creedence Clearwater Revival began to play out.

Philip bolted round.

Sarah fled through a door.

Philip gritted his teeth and gripped his gun. He headed through the door. Once through, he saw a stairwell that led up to a roof.

Bad Moon Rising continued to play out as Sarah made it to the roof.

She looked to the rooftop dance floor.

Lasers darted this way and that and holographic images of party-goers appeared.

It was a crowd and apart from strange glow around them, they were ever so realistic.

If you were a loner, fear not! You could have yourself an instant group of partying friends.

Sarah entered the holo-crowd just as Philip arrived. She weaved in and out of the virtual Japanese dancers and drinkers.

Below them, Brady had reached the Holo-Oke Bar. He looked around himself and heard 'Bad Moon Rising' escaping speakers from the rooftop. He was wary and his gun was tight in his left hand.

Lights flashed and swirled.

MEI'S ROCK PLAY LIST was visible on a digital screen.

"Credence to you, Mei." Brady mumbled. He noticed the stocks on the computer, then saw the eyeball on a counter. He checked the door and thought for a moment.

A laser ejected from somewhere and scanned Brady's eyes.

He blinked and curled his lip as the Robot Concierge spoke out.

"Yay! Welcome to the Holo-Oke Bar Joe Brady!"

Brady sank. "There goes the element of surprise."

Upon the roof, Philip titled his head and stepped through the virtual crowd.

Sarah became hopeful. She edged back to a low wall.

Neon signs illuminated the night behind her. Behind the wall were cables and wires and more rooftops and the city beyond.

She merged with the crowd.

Brady trod warily onto the rooftop terrace. He motioned for various realistic hologram people to get out the way. He frowned when they ignored him. "Get out the way. Ssh. Please. Move." He spotted a holographic bouncer and approached him. "Hey, get the people outta here will ya? -You hearing me, I said-" Brady waved his hand in front of the bouncer's face, which distorted. He bolted round at the people. He saw a dancer with a low cut top and reached out to touch her.. face.. "Yeah don't worry, assault is assault, even on a hologram person. Jesus."

BANG!

A gun sounded out.

Brady ducked amongst the holograms.

PUNCH!

Brady was hit in the head by Philip's fist. The force knocked him down to the floor.

Philip towered above him. He looked at his bloody fist and was disgusted by it.

"Wow! Your head is sticky and soft! I punched you where I shot you! Jesus! I thought my fist was going to go through your brain."

Brady was in severe pain. He turned over and tried tio crawl away.

Philip grabbed him. He pulled at his leg, yanking one shoe off, then a sock, revealing Brady's bare foot. Philip kicked Brady hard in the ribs and then crouched to Brady's level. "Joe Brady, look at yourself. You're a tired, bull-headed old man. A lone gunslinger, riding into a town where nobody wants you, doing what you think is best once again."

Brady was bloody and in utter pain. He was a broken man. He was worn like never before. "I guess old habits die hard." Brady spat blood.

Philip looked at him with disgust. "You will die."

"You'll die hardest."

Philip sneered. He stared at Brady, wincing, helpless.

"You know, there's a saying in Japan. Goes something like this. When I'm dead, my ghost is gonna hunt down and kill all your family's ghosts."

"I've not heard of that proverb. Is that a fact?" Philip was bemused.

"Well, not really, but it sounds kinda Japanese." Brady smiled through bloodied teeth.

Philip gritted his teeth and kicked Brady in the face. He stepped several feet away to the edge of the wall and checked his stocks on a digital device.

Sarah crawled through the virtual crowd towards her ex-husband, Brady. She cupped his bloody face. It was a complete mess. Sarah wiped blood from Brady's nose. "Joe? Joe, listen to me. It's Sarah. Can you hear me?" she began to cry. "Joe? Get up! Get up you old cowboy, get up!"

Philip turned. He squinted through the crowd and gripped his gun tightly.

Brady stired. He moaned. "This old cowboy's gettin up."

The Robot Concierge sounded out, excitedly. "Joe! You said cowboy. Lets find the hits that suit you best!"

Brady curled his lip.

Sarah smiled, with concerned relief.

BANG!

Sarah was suddenly shot in the chest! She was blasted backwards and forced down to the ground.

Brady was in total shock. He scowled at Philip. Enraged, he roared with absolute anger at seeing his true love on the tiled floor. With all his might and limited health, he pushed himself up. Brady raced towards Philip. He set foot into a run, pushing himself hard. He felt the tremendous pain in his arthritic hips and the bone rubbing against bone, due to the cartilage damage in his knees. He could even hear the sound of his discomfort. Like a worn brake pad on a car, metal grinding against metal, creating a disturbing squealing noise.

Another holographic image appeared.

It was Roy Rogers. He was in black and white and had a guitar in his hand. He began to sing 'I'm an old cowhand.'

The peculiar phrase 'Yippee-i-o-ki-ay' was sung.

Brady frowned. "Mother.. Fucker" Brady sighed with a combined disbelief and aggression. He continued to run and made contact with Philip. The force of impact was so hard Brady dislocated his shoulder and cracked his collarbone. The pain was unbearable that he felt like throwing up.

The sudden blow, blunt force trauma, to Philip's trachea – his windpipe, was crushed by the impact. As he was lifted off his feet, he hissed and frothed at the mouth. His lower jawbone disconnected and four teeth cracked and flew into the air as he was forced over the terrace wall. Philip smashed into an Oshiro neon sign and fizzled, as he received an almighty electric shock. He was stuck in the sign, smoldering. He was fiery and very dead. Charred flesh could be smelt as well as the scent of blood, smelling of metal. An only-child, it was said that Philip was the last of the avenging Muller-clan.

The Kitas had won. For generations they had been attacked by the Mullers, who sought to take their wealth, and suffered many casualties over the years. Had they betrayed the Mullers? Were the samurai who ambushed Jacob Muller and took his French rifles and Gatling guns really hired by the Kita family during the eighteen hundreds? If it weren't so, then why were the Mullers fueled with so much anger and absolute hatred and hell-bent on destroying them?

Brady toppled over the wall and became out of sight.

19. [nineteen]
The World On A String

Invented by a woman, Stephanie Kwolek, an American chemist created poly-paraphenylene terephthalamide, otherwise known as Kevlar, Norma and Technora. Kwolek first developed the material whilst working at DuPont in 1965. It was spun into high-strength fibers and became five-times stronger than steel. It was used as a replacement for steel in car tires, as well as in racing sails, bicycle tires and body armor. Stephanie Kwolek's invention had just saved a fellow sister's life.

Sarah coughed as she opened her shirt to reveal a bulletproof vest. It even had the Oshiro logo on it. She winced with pain and complete discomfort as she slowly got to her feet and walked to the wall. She looked over the wall.

Brady was tangled amongst the wires and cables. He was a complete mess and upside down.

Sarah assessed the utter danger of the situation. "Oh God, Joe. No. Please say you're alive. Please. You've come so far. Say you're alive. Goddammit, Joe, I'll remarry you if you'd just show me a sign you can hear me!"

Silence.

Sarah stared at his wreck of a body. Head to his..

Brady clenched the toes of his bare foot, making a fist.

Sarah smiled and began to sob. She cried with relief.

Brady held tight to a thin wire.

It was cutting his hand, slicing his palm and the inside of his fingers deeply.

His blood dripped down, but he held on tight, upside down.

"I've got the world on a string" by Sinatra began to play out.

Red and blue lights swirled in the night upon the bridge.

It was utter destruction.

There were fire crews. Police and medics tended to pretty much everything in sight.

Jaynus was being tended to by a beautiful Japanese medical tech outside the Oshiro Grand Plaza. The sight of her made him feel a lot better. "You've just made a very old man very happy." He gazed around his surrounds. The sight of destruction and chaos unsettled him and wondered about Brady. He felt all right, secure. Jaynus nodded to himself and tried to remain positive. If Brady was dead, then so be it, it was meant to be and perhaps a most suited outcome for everyone involved. If he was alive, then that was cool, too. Despite the argumentative and dangerous nature of their relationship, Jaynus preferred the latter. He would miss his old friend, Brady, if he weren't around anymore. In the distance, he saw an electrical spark from a neon sign. Jaynus smiled and focused on his wounds.

The Kita Clan were approached by Inspector Edogawa and Detective Rampo, with a handful of uniformed cops who tailed behind them.

Edogawa knew deep down that the Kita's family business was affiliated with the yakuza.

For many, it would be difficult to believe that the Oshiro Corporation wasn't involved in some sort of organized crime. How could a global super-brand reach such great heights without a little help from some gangster persuasion?

From the shatei, little brothers on the street, applying pressure on the local street vendors, selling and promoting Oshiro goods instead of rival products, to the first lieutenants, the wakagashira, taking a more threatening, suit-wearing stance in business. The yakuza were involved in many a business venture, be it a small or large-scale operation.

The Oshiro Corporation had been hit hard before. Oshiro roughly translated to mean 'big castle'. Like every castle, they were prone to being besieged. It wasn't the first time, the Kita castle had been attacked and it certainly wasn't the last.

The glistening of the water, the glow of neon, the swirling emergency lights and the twinkling of a smoking Oshiro sign all blended into one another.

It was a disaster zone.

"I've got the world on a string" belted out into the night.

[e]pilogue

The press reporting on the many scandals that tied their business to the yakuza hit the Oshiro Corporation hard.

The Kita family could take the financial punch, however it was the public embarrassment, which affected them, most. They prided themselves on being a clean-cut family-run business, adored by a nation, let alone a city. Their banking service, Oshiro Money, was investigated and was revealed to be loaning the money to the yakuza.

The Oshiro investigation led to a number of other high profile Japanese banks being looked into. They each had yakuza ties.

Loan payments, however, were very difficult to collect from the mafia.

The Kita-clan mourned their losses and vowed to bounce back, promising to one another they would be bigger and better than ever before.

Although she remained on the board, Sarah Kita received an undisclosed retirement package from Oshiro. Professionally, she conducted charity work, in the US and Japan, under the name Sarah Kita, however her official name was Sarah Brady.

Jaynus Carter continued to live in New York City. He opened several stores around the City and in other states and stores in London and Europe. He was given sole trading rights and his stores would be the official seller of Oshiro products worldwide. A flagship store was opened in Tokyo, but Jaynus did not attend its opening. He instead appeared via a live video link. It would be the first shop of its kind to be entirely run by robotic 'employees'.

Eve Brady patched things up with her boyfriend Dan Simmons. She gave birth to a healthy baby boy and named him Joseph. Eve married Dan in a beautifully romantic ceremony at Belhurst Castle, on the shores of Seneca Lake, in Upstate New York. Among the guests were of course her brother, Ben and also Private investigator Ed Williams, Jaynus Carter, Diamond Thorp and naturally her mother, Sarah.

Her father, Joe, gave her away.

[a]bout
the author

Ben Trebilcook was born and raised in London, England. Due to strong family connections in New York and in London, he grew up around the world of law enforcement and secret intelligence, fields of which feature prominently in all aspects of his writing. Ben has worked in the film industry for twenty years, predominantly in screenwriting. He balances his film work with teaching disaffected, disadvantaged young people in South-east London.

His first novel, a thriller fusing the worlds of education and espionage, entitled 'My Name Is Not Jacob Ramsay', is available on Kindle and in paperback via Amazon.

Printed in Great Britain
by Amazon